THE
WEiRD
CLUB

THE SEARCH FOR
THE JERSEY DEVIL

STERLING
New York / London
www.sterlingpublishing.com

Mark Moran and Mark Sceurman,
authors of *Weird U.S.*, present

THE WEIRD CLUB

THE SEARCH FOR THE JERSEY DEVIL

by Randy Fairbanks

Published by Sterling Publishing Co., Inc.
387 Park Avenue South, New York, NY 10016

© 2007 by Randy Fairbanks, Mark Moran, and Mark Sceurman

Distributed in Canada by Sterling Publishing
c/o Canadian Manda Group, 165 Dufferin Street,
Toronto, Ontario, Canada M6K 3H6
Distributed in the United Kingdom by GMC Distribution Services,
Castle Place, 166 High Street, Lewes, East Sussex, England BN7 1XU
Distributed in Australia by Capricorn Link (Australia) Pty. Ltd.
P.O. Box 704, Windsor, NSW 2756, Australia

ISBN 13: 978-1-4027-4228-6
ISBN 10: 1-4027-4228-2

2 4 6 8 10 9 7 5 3 1

For information about custom editions, special sales, premium and
corporate purchases, please contact Sterling Special Sales
Department at 800-805-5489 or specialsales@sterlingpub.com.

Design: Richard J. Berenson
        Berenson Design & Books, LLC, New York, NY

To my father, who sometimes
wears gym socks on his hands.

Contents

Chapter #1
The Weird Club Begins!

Hello, my name is Mark Aldrich and I have a club called the Weird Club. So far, I'm the only member. That means I'm the president and vice-president, as well as the treasurer. My older sister, Michelle, says that it's weird to have a club where you're the only member. So I said, "Fine! Then I'll call it the Weird Club!" That's how my club got its name.

The purpose of the Weird Club is to look for local legends about ghosts or monsters, creepy tales of UFOs and space aliens, bizarre buildings, spooky cemeteries, or even just odd people who live nearby. I'm fascinated by anything that's unusual or remarkable, mysterious, unexplainable, or just plain weird!

I told my family all about it during dinner last night. Michelle stared at me the whole time. So did my younger sister, Rachel.

"Nobody's going to want to be in a club like that!" snapped Michelle.

"It sounds weird," said Rachel, chewing her spaghetti.

"Of course it's weird!" I replied. "That's the whole point!"

But my father thought it was interesting . . . and he gave me this journal so I could keep track of my club's findings.

So now I have a Weird Club journal. I even have a Weird Club logo! Here's what it looks like:

Pretty cool, huh?

LET ME TELL YOU about how I started my club. It all began with a photo that I took on a class trip last month.

I live in New Jersey, in a town called Basking Ridge. It's mainly famous for its rolling hills, which means that there's not much to do here. It's just a pretty small, pretty normal place. But like most places that seem normal at first, you can find a lot of weird stuff going on. You just have to look for it.

My seventh-grade class went on a trip to a place called Jockey Hollow, in nearby Morristown. George Washington and his soldiers camped out there during the Revolutionary War. Our teacher, Mr. Dorman, said they stayed there during the coldest winter in over 100 years, and many men died.

I shivered. It was a gray, gloomy day. I glanced around the campgrounds and saw some small timber huts, which were made to look like the huts that the soldiers used. The huts were kind of spooky, so I took some pictures with my digital camera.

Later on, when I looked at the photos, I noticed something weird.

Here's a really neat combination fork and knife that was used by one of Washington's men at Jockey Hollow over 200 years ago!

9

This is the photo with the strange ball of light in front of the cabin.

In one shot, hovering a few feet above the ground in front of a hut, was a strange ball of light. I knew I hadn't seen anything like that at the campgrounds. Mr. Dorman said that it was just the glare from the sun, but the day wasn't sunny at all.

So what was it? Was this floating light in my photo the spirit of one of the men who had died during the nasty winter at Jockey Hollow? Or was it just a problem with my camera? I can't say for sure, but the mystery behind that picture really hooked me!

THAT WEEK, I joined the photography club at school.

"Your pictures need work, Mark," lectured Mrs. Moyes, the math teacher who ran the photography club. "Don't rush when you photograph. Take time and frame the shot properly."

But I didn't care about framing at all. In my pictures, I was hunting for ghost lights and phantom shapes!

After school, I sat at my computer and did a search: "Ghost hunting." I got over 300,000 hits, so I knew that I wasn't the only person out there interested in this stuff. I learned that lots of people use photographs to hunt for evidence of ghosts. On one web page, I learned that ghost hunters have words to describe the ball of light in the picture I took at Jockey Hollow. They call it an *orb* or an *aura*. Ghost hunters have special words for everything. If something is unexplainable and mysterious, they call it *paranormal*. They even have a word for the glowing slime that ghosts leave behind. They call it *ectoplasm*. Yuck!

Some ghost hunters carry tape recorders. They believe that ghosts are trying to communicate with us, but our ears aren't sensitive enough to hear what they're saying. We can only hear them by using electronic equipment.

Wow! Tape recordings of ghosts talking!

I was curious, so I downloaded some of these recordings and I played them on my computer. I don't know if the sounds were actually made by spirits or if they were just fakes, but I got creeped out just listening to them. These weird recordings are called *EVPs*. That stands for "Electronic Voice Phenomena."

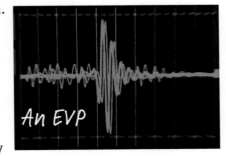
An EVP

I dug up an old tape recorder from the basement and brought it with me when the photography

The old ballroom at Phareloch Castle

club went to Phareloch Castle last week. That's a building in Basking Ridge that they say is haunted. While the other students posed for photos in an arched stone doorway, I took lots of pictures of the dark, quiet corners of the old ballroom, hoping to capture more ghostly images on film.

Then I took out my tape recorder. "What on earth are you recording?" asked Mrs. Moyes when she saw me holding my microphone up to the rough stone wall.

"EVPs," I explained. "That stands for 'Electronic Voice Phenomena.' I'm trying to record the ghost of Phareloch Castle!"

After that, Mrs. Moyes kicked me out of the photography club. She said that I was scaring the other students.

THAT'S WHEN I DECIDED to start a club of my own. I was hoping that I could get some other people to join, too. There are far too many strange places, people, and stories for me to write about them all.

I went to the principal's office during study hall yesterday and asked Mr. Alpert, the principal, about it. He looked at me from behind his cluttered desk.

"In order for the school to officially recognize a club, all you need to do is sign up at least five members," he said.

"Five members," I repeated, disappointed.

He said, "Sure, just ask some friends of yours to join."

Unfortunately, I don't really have a whole lot of friends. So the principal suggested that I make an announcement in class.

This morning, my homeroom teacher, Mrs. Fishetti, called me to the front of the classroom. "Mark has a wonderful surprise for you," she said. "He's starting a club and he wants to tell you all about it. Maybe you'll find it so interesting that you'll all want to join."

My classmates learn about the Weird Club

I walked up to her desk and looked out at the other kids. They were all watching me. I was nervous, so I started talking really fast.

"I'm starting a club called the Weird Club," I explained. "The purpose of the Weird Club is to look for anything that's unusual or remarkable, mysterious, unexplainable, or just plain weird!"

Excited, I talked about paranormal research and I showed my classmates the floating orb in the picture from Jockey Hollow. I showed them my tape recorder and I told them about EVPs. Then I asked if anyone was interested in joining the club. Everyone stayed quiet. No hands went up.

Later, in the cafeteria line, I heard Wendy Williams talking to her friends. She's super-popular and totally stuck-up.

"Who'd want to join a club like that?" she said. "Floating balls of light! Electronic Ghost Phenomena!"

"It's not Electronic Ghost Phenomena," I corrected her. "It's E-V-P. It stands for 'Electronic Voice Phenomena.'"

Wendy rolled her eyes. Her friends rolled their eyes too.

"Whatever!" she replied, giggling. "The point is that no one wants to join your weirdo club!"

The day only got worse from there. On the way home, Ricky and Tim Solkin followed behind me. I started walking faster. You have to watch out for the Solkin Twins—they're the school bullies. They have no friends because everyone is afraid of them. They're tall and mean, with wild eyes and long, messy red hair.

"What do you have there, Weirdo?" Ricky demanded. He grabbed my tape recorder and threw it to Tim. I lunged for it but missed, and it smashed on the sidewalk. "Oops!" said Tim, laughing. I was furious, but what could I do? They're bigger than me.

When I got home, I checked out the tape recorder. At first, it didn't work. But after I gave it a couple of shakes, it started running. So I guess it's okay.

I'M STILL HOPING that some kids will join my club, so I decided to make a poster and put it up in school. It will include my address and phone number along with information about club meetings.

I'm going to hold them in my room on Wednesday afternoons. Maybe someone will see the poster and will come to the next meeting. If not, a club is still a club even if it only has one member. At least, I think so.

The WEIRD CLUB

JOIN TODAY!

Meetings every Wednesday 3:30 to 5 p.m.

Mark Aldrich, President
Basking Ridge Road
Basking Ridge, NJ
908 555-7346

Chapter #2
The Jersey Devil

It's Wednesday afternoon, meeting time, and I have a great story for my Weird Club journal today! Last weekend, I went with my family to South Jersey to visit my grandparents. They live in a place called Leisureville. I think it's only for retired people. On the surface, Leisureville doesn't seem like a spooky place.

Hold on, I take that back. There is a strange woman named Mrs. White who lives across the street from my grandparents. She's always out walking. Every time I see her, she's wandering up and down the street or through the woods. It's like she's looking for something that she can't find. And she always dresses all in white. I think she looks like a ghost, but my grandmother says that she's just a lonely old lady.

Other than Mrs. White, I've never noticed anything spooky about Leisureville. It's a quiet, calm neighborhood, where most of the houses look alike. The old people who live there wave and smile whenever we pass them on the street. But Leisureville is right next to one of the spookiest places in all of New Jersey: a thick forest called the Pine Barrens.

For nearly 300 years, people have been telling stories about a strange creature that lives in the Pine Barrens. Not many people have actually *seen* the creature, but those who have seen it say that it has the head of a dog, the body of a kangaroo, and wings like a giant bat. And that's not all—it also has antlers like a deer, the face of a horse, two legs like a human, a long, forked lizard tail, and two extremely sharp, threatening claws. Sounds like a whole zoo in one monster!

This hodgepodge beast of the New Jersey Pine Barrens is known as the Jersey Devil.

theory may explain how the legend ties in with an actual monster; some people believe that around the time that the hidden deformed child was discover people began sightings of a beast and put the stor together. There are other tales that suggest Leeds herself was a witch or that she was cursed by loca for having an affair with a British soldier. The Shrouds House, a log cabin within the Pine Barre was reputed to be the birthplace of the Devil. O ruins of the foundation of the house and a few parts still exist today.

The Jersey Devil has been said to be compa to a headless pirate, a ghostly woman, and a we wolf. In certain parts of South Jersey, the Devil mored to live in an apocryphal Agent Orange near Chatsworth, a very small town surrounde forest and sand.

There is another description of the devil that well-known to local people in South Jersey. A in South Jersey was having her first baby and wanted him to be perfect. When the baby w it was the most ugly looking baby that anyo ever seen at that time. The mother was so u she said "This isn't my son. This is the devi May God give the thing back to him!" Afte this, she threw her son into the river. The Now that river is said to be haunted by the Many people have died there. It is said th an unknown source which sucks air to it f a rock. When people swim near there, th sucked under the rock; they are then hel they die. Once they are dead, the body i that it floats to the top for everyone to needed]

Native American legends told of the de ly being that protected the Pines. Sight devil were believed to be signs of good view was widely accepted by locals fro 1700s until 1909.

According to one version of the tale, Mitch Biwer was thirteenth child born to a Mother Leeds, a resident of the Pine Barrens in 1735. Mother Leeds was so upset at yet another pregnancy that after giving birth she exclaimed, "I am tired of children! Let the devil take this one!" What was once a human child immediately transformed into winged monstrosity; he ate all the other children and flew out through the chimney. There are many versions of this legend, differing in date of the birth and the degree of the Devil's disfigurement. In some stories, the Devil is merely a human child which Mother Leeds confined to her cellar or attic, only to have it escape into the woods (see feral children for more on similar legends and real life examples). A fork on this

Talk about a great hiding place! The Pine Barrens cover over a million acres. They're thick and mysterious and so dark that no crops can grow there. That's why they're called "barren." But lots of deer and bear and fox live there—so why not the Jersey Devil?

And did I mention that it's six feet tall? And did I mention that the Pine Barrens are right in my grandparents' backyard? Maybe Leisureville is not such a restful place after all!

Before our trip to Leisureville, I checked out a book about the Pine Barrens from the school library. I read it in the car on the way there, and I learned a lot about the Jersey Devil.

According to the legend, in 1735 a poor woman known as Mother Leeds, who had 12 children, learned that she was expecting another. Afraid that she could not take care of a 13th, she threw up her hands in fear and said, "Let this one be a devil!"

Her neighbors were shocked by this horrible wish.

On the stormy night that Mother Leeds gave birth, she was surrounded by women from the town—some there to help, others just curious.

At first, the baby seemed to be a normal little boy. Many of the women watching were disappointed. But suddenly, the child morphed, sprouting claws, wings, fur, and feathers. Its eyes glowed red as it grew bigger and bigger until it seemed to fill the room. As the women watched in terror, the monster baby killed its own mother! Then it attacked the others, tearing them to shreds with its sharp claws. Not all of them died. Some were horribly injured but remained alive to see the creature blast up through the chimney, destroying it on the way. They say it let out a horrible shriek and disappeared into the darkness of the Pine Barrens.

"HAVE YOU EVER HEARD of the Jersey Devil?" I asked my grandmother and grandfather when we got to Leisureville.

"What's that?" replied Grampa.

"It's a monster. And supposedly, it lives in the woods behind your house."

Grandma left the room because she doesn't like scary stories. Then I told Grampa all about the Jersey Devil.

"You believe that story?" laughed Grampa. "Sounds like supernatural hogwash to me!"

I should tell you that Grampa is a retired electrical engineer. As a scientist, he was skeptical about a baby turning into a horse-faced, flying dragon.

Still, I think he looked a little shaken. He kept glancing out the window toward the Pine Barrens.

Finally, he said that sometimes at night, when it's really quiet, he hears a strange animal crying in the forest. "I don't think it's the Jersey Devil," Grampa said. "But something's definitely out there."

That afternoon, Grampa and I explored the woods together. It was cold outside, so Grampa wore gym socks on his hands. He never uses gloves. He says that gym socks are easier, because he never has to look for a matching pair or think about which hand goes in which glove. And to protect himself against ticks in the forest, he put rubber bands around his jacket sleeves and pants legs. He looked pretty silly, but I'm used to the funny way he dresses.

"You're going outside like that?" my grandmother asked when she saw Grampa. "You look ridiculous." But she was smiling.

As we walked in the woods, Grampa softly whistled "Jingle Bells." It's his favorite song to whistle, no matter what season it is. That's another weird habit of his.

It felt kind of creepy walking down the trail, especially after reading about the Jersey Devil. The late afternoon sun barely made it through the thick trees, and I wished we had brought a flashlight, even though it was daytime. Soon we had left the houses far behind, and there were no other people in sight. I jumped every time I heard a sound.

21

We walked for a few minutes, but we didn't see any animal big-ger than a squirrel. Finally, Grampa said, "I probably should get you back. Isn't it dinnertime by now?" It was only five o'clock, but I was relieved to go back. The Pine Barrens stretch on for miles, and I was afraid we might get lost.

So we walked back to my grandparents' house, and we gave up on our search for the Jersey Devil. For now.

Chapter #3
A Ride on Gravity Hill

Today, I had three cavities filled. My face is still numb but I'm in a good mood because I cut a deal with my mother. I would go to the dentist *and* go clothes-shopping with my sisters. But afterwards, we would all do something that I like to do. It had to be something really good to make up for all of that!

So my mom took us to Gravity Hill.

There are gravity hills, also called gravity *roads,* all over the country, maybe even all over the world. If someone drives to a gravity road and puts the car into neutral, the car will drift slowly *up* the hill, against gravity. Each gravity road has its own story, but from the stuff I've read, the stories seem pretty similar from place to place. Each spot was the scene of a horrible death, or sometimes even a murder. And the spirit of the victim has never moved on. The legends claim that the ghost is pushing or pulling the car up the hill.

The gravity road closest to me is at a stop sign off an exit of Route 208 in Bergen County, New Jersey. According to the story, a long time ago a woman was killed at that intersection. They say her ghost continues to haunt the spot, trying to protect people from having the same thing happen to them.

Before I tell you what happened when I went to Gravity Hill, let me stop for a second. Since I keep mentioning my family, I guess I should let you know what they're like.

MY MOM and dad are okay, except they won't let me take my video camera to the cemetery at midnight to film the mysterious glowing gravestone (maybe I'll tell you about it another time). My mother works in the town library, which might explain why I love old books. And my father is a physicist for the U.S. government. His work is top secret. He can't even tell me about it.

"Does it involve radiation?" I ask him. "Spy planes? Mind control?"

But he never answers. He just sits there with a sly smile on his face. One thing I like about my father: he's very mysterious.

I also have two sisters. I already told you about them.

Alright,
now you know
my family, so we
can get back to the
story. . . .

"WHY DO THEY call it
Gravity Hill, anyway?"
said Michelle as we
approached the haunted
intersection in our old car.
"It makes no sense! They
should call it Anti-gravity Hill!"

My mom pulled over to the curb and I jumped out of the car with my Weird Club kit. It's actually just a backpack with my camera and tape recorder and a few other things. Luckily, I'd remembered to bring a container of baby powder too—a good thing to have for collecting evidence. Ghost hunters say that if a spirit touches a surface covered in baby powder, flour, or dust, it will leave behind a ghostly handprint!

"What are you doing?" asked my mother.

"Putting baby powder on the car," said Michelle, rolling her eyes.

"It's for ghost prints," I told them. "Don't you know anything?"

"Mark, can I help?" asked Rachel, climbing out to join me.

I showed Rachel how to sprinkle baby powder evenly all over the hood and the bumpers. Mom and Michelle stayed inside the car and watched us work.

"Is that enough?" asked Rachel. Her hair and clothes were as powdered as the car.

"It's perfect!"

Then I looked back up the hill. A few vehicles passed us, heading down the ramp. When the coast was clear, Rachel and I hopped back into the car.

"Okay, Mom. Put it into neutral and take your foot off the brake."

She did. Normally, putting a car in neutral would make it roll down the hill. But instead, we began to slowly travel *up* the hill, seemingly against gravity.

My mom and I grinned. Rachel giggled. Of course, Michelle wasn't impressed.

"It's an optical illusion," she insisted. "There's no ghost! It looks like we're going uphill, but we're really going downhill!"

"Maybe," I said, holding up the baby powder. "Or maybe, we'll get ghost prints on the car. That would be evidence of spectral phenomena."

"'Spectral phenomena'?" Michelle groaned. "Give me a break!"

"That's a phrase that ghost hunters use," I told her. "It means 'ghosts.'"

"Why don't they just say 'ghosts'?" asked Rachel.

"'Ghost hunters'!" said Michelle. "Baby powder! Why do I have such a weirdo for a brother?"

I couldn't wait to check for ghost prints. Unfortunately, as we were picking up speed, rolling backward up the hill, a police car showed up, flashing its lights. As my mother pulled over and rolled down the window, we saw a sign outside which read:

TRYING OUT GRAVITY ROAD
IS NOT PERMITTED

After getting a ticket, my mother was so mad that she wouldn't let me check for ghost prints. Then, on the way home, it started raining, so all remaining evidence, if there was any, was washed away.

I was disappointed that I didn't get to check for ghost prints. But it was still really great going up Gravity Hill (or Anti-gravity Hill, if you ask Michelle). Too bad my mom won't ever take me back there.

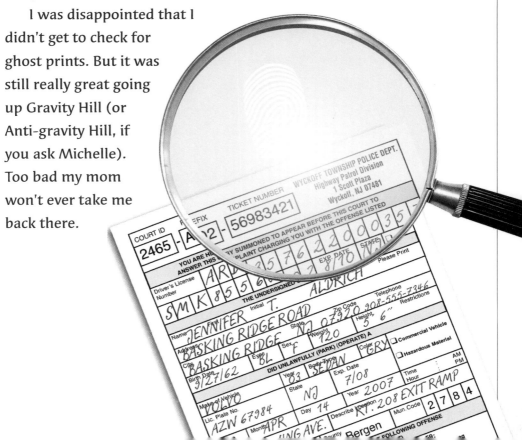

Chapter #4
Spookiness in San Antonio

Exciting news! This afternoon, just as I was about to start my Wednesday Weird Club meeting, my mom knocked on my door.

"Mark, there's a boy standing on the porch. I asked him if he wanted something, but he didn't answer. I think he's just shy. Maybe he wants to talk to you."

I went downstairs and opened the front door. It was a kid from school, Mark Brownlow. He's new in town and I don't really know him that well. He's kind of funny-looking—short and chubby, with lots of freckles.

"Hey, what's up?" I said.

He just stood there on the doorstep, rocking back and forth. My mom was right. He's shy. Super shy.

I tried again. "I know you from school, right? Your name is Mark, just like mine."

The other Mark nodded. Unable to look me in the eye, he stared down at his sneakers. Finally, he managed a few words.

"I . . . I . . . uh . . . "

He tried again. "I . . . I saw your poster at school," he muttered, holding up a crumpled flier. "Can I join your club?"

I smiled and then I laughed. "Really?" I asked him. I couldn't believe that someone was finally taking my club seriously. "You really want to join?" I was so happy that I felt like jumping up and down.

And I found out he really did want to join! He wasn't even so shy anymore once we started talking. It turns out he moved here last year, from San Antonio, Texas.

So let me introduce Mark, the newest member of the Weird Club. Alright—so you don't get us mixed up, since my last name starts with an A and his last name starts with a B—we'll call ourselves Mark A and Mark B. Now maybe my sister will stop bugging me about having a club with only one member!

To the Weird Club:

Hello, fans of the Weird! My name is Mark B and I grew up in San Antonio, Texas. When I first heard about the Weird Club, I immediately thought of my hometown. You can't get weirder than San Antonio! It's haunted! At least, that's what they say.

Ghosts are my favorite subject. I also like history because ghosts and history go together. Do you think ghosts are real? Or are they just in our imaginations? And, if they do exist, what are they? Are they confused spirits of people who died sudden deaths, so that they don't even know that they're dead? Or are they just too stubborn to accept that their life on Earth is over?

Of course, you don't have to answer any of these questions. That's one of the great things about ghost stories. They ask a lot of questions that no one can answer.

The Donkey Lady

One of the weirdest San Antonio ghost stories is about the Donkey Lady.

"The Donkey Lady's gonna get you!" my brother used to shout, to frighten me. "The Donkey Lady's gonna get you!" Then he'd make crazy "hee-haw" noises. It always terrified me. I guess it was pretty easy to scare me back then.

So, what is the Donkey Lady? Well, it's hard to say for sure, because there are so many different stories about her.

In one, the Donkey Lady is the angry ghost of a woman who died in a horrible car accident. The skin of her face hangs loose and her fingers are all melted together so that her hands resemble hooves. Weird!

The stories get even weirder. I heard that if you go to a certain area of San Antonio and you hide in the bushes and make "hee-haw" sounds, then the Donkey Lady will appear. In this version, she's a monster with the body of a woman and a hideous donkey head!

But in my favorite version of the legend, the Donkey Lady was a woman whose best friend was a donkey. Every day, she would stroll with her donkey on Applewhite Road and they'd cross the bridge over Elm Creek to get to a grassy field where the donkey would graze. People would make fun of the Donkey Lady because they all thought she was weird. She just ignored them.

Donkey Lady Bridge

Then one day, a boy who lived nearby made up a terrible lie. He told his father that the donkey had bitten him. The boy's father decided that the donkey had to go. He hid near the bridge with several other men and, when the woman walked by, they jumped out and grabbed the donkey's rope. They tried to take the donkey, but the lady struggled against them. She hugged her donkey so tightly that the men couldn't pry her loose. As she held on, the frightened animal reared back and lost its balance. Together, the two fell off the bridge.

And so, on that sad day, the woman and the donkey drowned in Elm Creek.

The bridge is now called Donkey Lady Bridge. People say if you drive there and turn off your car's headlights, then the ghost of the Donkey Lady will think that you've come to take her donkey away. She'll get angry and start throwing rocks. Then you'll hear the sound of hooves coming closer and closer. . . .

My father said that when he was a teenager he would park with his friends on Donkey Lady Bridge and wait for her to show up. Once, on the empty bridge at night, they heard the click–clack sound of the phantom donkey approaching.

I asked him what happened next.

He just laughed and said, "We didn't wait around to find out."

The Ghosts of the Alamo

Here's another weird story from Texas. . . .

A few years ago, we took a class trip to the Alamo, a place that's famous for its history and for its ghosts. And as we walked through the old buildings, the tour guide told us the history.

"It's most famous as the site of the bloody Battle of the Alamo," he explained. "American colonists in Texas were fighting for independence from Mexico. Two hundred Texan fighters were attacked by thousands of Mexican soldiers. The Texans turned the Alamo into a fortress. From inside these strong walls, they held off the soldiers for 13 days. Finally, the fortress fell and the rebellious Texans, the brave defenders of the Alamo, were all killed."

As the guide spoke, I imagined the battle happening around me. I pictured people dying right where I was standing.

I shuddered. The Alamo was giving me the willies. It felt haunted, just like I had heard. I wondered if it really *was* haunted. I raised my hand to ask the tour guide.

"Can I help you?" he asked.

I nodded. All the people in the tour group were watching me.

"Well?" he said, waiting. "What is it?"

"I . . . I . . . uh . . ."

Finally, I blurted out my question. "Are there ghosts here?"

"Ghosts?" The tour guide grinned. "Of course there are ghosts! The Alamo is the number-one most ghost-filled, haunted place in the United States!"

The tour guide loved to talk about the ghosts. This was definitely the best part of the class trip. "When the Battle of the Alamo was over," he said, "the Mexican army had a huge problem

on their hands. Do you know what it was?"

I shook my head no.

"They didn't know what to do with all those dead bodies," he told us. "There were so many corpses that it was impossible to bury them all. So, some of the bodies were burned. And others were just tossed in the San Antonio River. Since they weren't buried properly, the dead could not rest in peace. That's why, ever since then, the Alamo has been haunted. The ghosts protected the fortress! So when the Mexican troops were ordered to destroy the Alamo, they ran away instead. They said that fiery spirits appeared and spoke to them.

"'Do not touch the Alamo! Do not touch these walls!'" he moaned, acting out the ghosts' warning.

"And the same ghosts are still here?" I asked, breathless.

"That's right," he said. "In the cemetery. In the barracks. In the gift shop. They wander the Alamo, wounded and bleeding, looking for someone to help them."

When the tour was over, we returned to the school bus. I looked around the grounds one more time, hoping to spot a ghost. I almost jumped out of my seat when I saw someone in an old colonial soldier's uniform, limping across the parking lot.

It was probably just a tourist.

But you never really know. Not at the Alamo.

More weirdness to come!

—Mark B

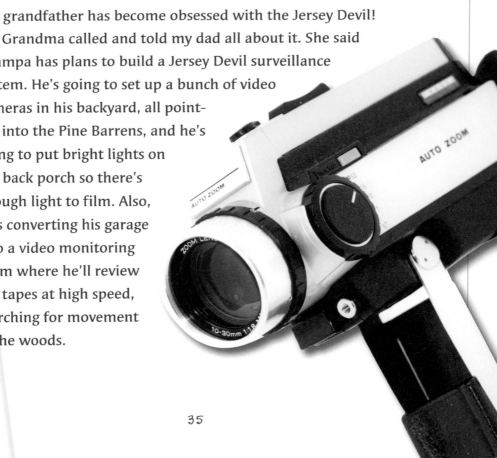

Chapter #5
Jersey Devil Update

Mark A here.

My grandfather has become obsessed with the Jersey Devil!

Grandma called and told my dad all about it. She said Grampa has plans to build a Jersey Devil surveillance system. He's going to set up a bunch of video cameras in his backyard, all pointing into the Pine Barrens, and he's going to put bright lights on the back porch so there's enough light to film. Also, he's converting his garage into a video monitoring room where he'll review the tapes at high speed, searching for movement in the woods.

"Thanks for giving your grandfather a hobby!" Grandma said during our phone call. I couldn't tell if she was annoyed or amused. "Well," she sighed. "At least it's keeping him busy."

That night, I was too excited to sleep, so I wrote an email to Grampa.

```
To: JingleBells@weirdclub.com
Hi Grampa,

Do you really think you'll find the Jersey
Devil? When are you setting up your Jersey Devil
surveillance system? Can I come and help?

☺ Mark
```

The next morning, he wrote back.

```
To: MarkA@weirdclub.com

Maybe. Saturday. Yes.

Love,
Grampa
```

That's another weird thing about Grampa. He writes very short emails.

Chapter #6
The Search for the Jersey Devil Begins

I got up early on Saturday morning. I bolted out of bed and got dressed in a flash. Then I woke up my father.

"C'mon Dad! We have to go help Grampa build his Jersey Devil surveillance system!"

"Oh, I forgot. Today's Jersey Devil Day," mumbled my father as he got out of bed. "You know, the New Jersey Devils are a hockey team. Only in New Jersey would they name a hockey team after a horse-faced, flying dragon."

WHEN WE ARRIVED in Leisureville, Grampa was working in the backyard, spacing rocks evenly apart right where the woods began.

"Hey!" he called out when he saw us. "You're just in time. I've figured out where the umbrellas are going to go."

"Umbrellas?" I asked.

"Of course!" replied Grampa, pointing to a pile of beach umbrellas on the small back porch. "These will protect the video cameras from the sun and the rain. Now, no dawdling! Let's get to work!"

My dad and I drove beach umbrellas into the spots that Grampa had marked, and Grampa followed behind, fastening a video camera to each umbrella.

It was hard work, so when my grandmother brought out a pitcher of lemonade, Dad and I took a break while Grampa continued working. As we sipped our drinks, I noticed that we were being watched by a frail old man with red hair and a goofy smile. Grampa said it was his next-door neighbor, Mr. Bice.

Grampa's video-umbrellas

"Whatcha workin' on?" asked Mr. Bice, peering out his back door.

"We're setting up video cameras to monitor the woods," I said. "There's a strange animal out there and we have reason to believe that it's the Jersey Devil."

Mr. Bice smiled. "The Jersey Devil, huh?" he said. Using a walker, he slowly made his way across his yard and headed over to us. His hands were shaky, so the walker jiggled as he moved. "You know, in West Virginia, where I'm from, we had our own flying monster. A big, brown thing with wings. They called it Mothman!"

"Really?" I exclaimed. "Mothman?"

"Forget about Mothman!" interrupted Grampa. "Let's concentrate on the Jersey Devil. And no more gabbing. We have umbrellas to plant!"

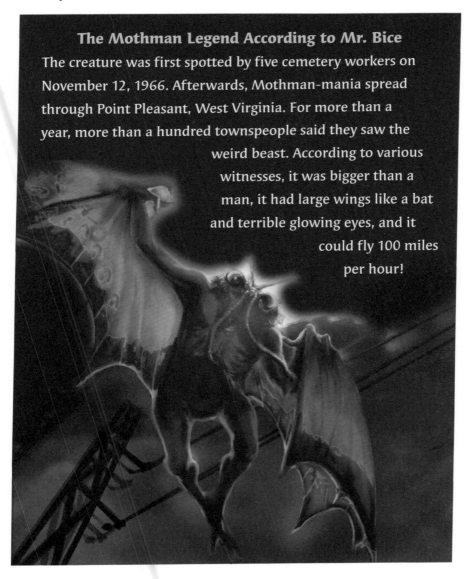

The Mothman Legend According to Mr. Bice

The creature was first spotted by five cemetery workers on November 12, 1966. Afterwards, Mothman-mania spread through Point Pleasant, West Virginia. For more than a year, more than a hundred townspeople said they saw the weird beast. According to various witnesses, it was bigger than a man, it had large wings like a bat and terrible glowing eyes, and it could fly 100 miles per hour!

Break time was over. My dad and I got back to work and Mr. Bice helped out. He moved really slowly, but he did the best he could, and I could tell that Grampa appreciated it.

BY THE END OF THE AFTERNOON, we were finished. Grampa and I grabbed videotapes and loaded the cameras. We powered them up and then stepped back and watched the red lights flashing. We were recording! If the Jersey Devil made an appearance, we would get it on tape!

After that, my dad barbecued hot dogs on the gas grill and Mr. Bice joined us. It was the perfect way to begin our search for the Jersey Devil. And it was nice to see Grampa laughing with Mr. Bice. My grampa doesn't have many friends. Since he's kind of cranky and he dresses funny, people usually stay clear of him.

As the sun went down, we sat there on the porch and traded stories about bizarre beasts and ghosts. Mr. Bice told us that sometimes, at night, he hears his wife walking around the house, turning the TV on and off. But she died ten years ago!

"Spooky," I said. "Could I go in your house sometime and get EVPs?"

"EVPs!" scoffed Grampa. "You and your ghosts."

"You don't believe in ghosts?" I asked.

"I'm skeptical," replied Grampa. "I'm also skeptical about the Jersey Devil, but if there's something weird sneaking around in the woods behind my house, I want to know what it is."

Grampa gazed into the woods for a moment. With a grin, he grabbed his lemonade and held it up high.

"Whatever it is," he declared. "If it's out there, we'll find it!"
We all clinked our glasses together and repeated his toast.
"If it's out there, we'll find it!"

Chapter #7
A Gross Love Story from Florida

Well, it looks like my club with no members is growing every day.
Mark B said his cousin Diana loved the idea of the Weird Club.
She's 13 and lives in Key West, Florida. He gave her my email
address. He also showed me a picture of her.

"Wow!" I said. "She looks like a vampire!"

Mark B laughed. "Nuh-uh, she's just Goth."

I didn't know what Goth was, so I searched on the internet,
and I saw some pictures of other people who were
Goth. They looked
like vampires too. I
guess, if you're Goth,
you're supposed to
look that way.

A few days later,
I got an email from
Mark's cousin with
a story for the Weird
Club journal.

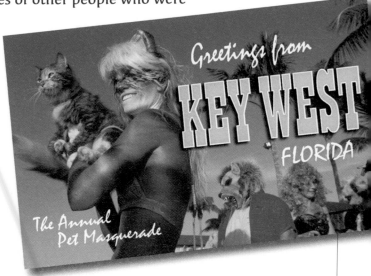

Greetings from
KEY WEST
FLORIDA
The Annual Pet Masquerade

To the Weird Club:

Greetings, my dear Mark. My cousin (the other Mark) says you're cool. If you ever find yourself in Florida, come for a visit. Just don't ever say that I look like a vampire again. :) Heh, heh. Sorry my cousin is such a blabbermouth. Better be careful what you say around him.

I submit to you the grisly legend of Count Carl von Cosel and the love of his life, Elena Milagro Hoyos Mesa. (Ya gotta love these names!)

Count Carl was an eccentric old inventor who worked as a technician in an X-ray lab in Key West, Florida. He fell in love with one of his patients, a beautiful 20-year-old girl named Elena. Sadly, Elena soon died of tuberculosis, but that didn't stop Count Carl from loving her . . . or from wanting to be with her.

Okay, now this is where the story starts to get kind of gross!

Count Carl felt that if he could perfectly preserve Elena's corpse, then he could somehow resurrect her. First he put her body in a special coffin that sprayed her body with formaldehyde, a preservative. He placed a telephone inside the coffin so

Count Carl von Cosel admiring Elena's photo

that he could talk with Elena's corpse. He was kind of insane, don't you think?

Then he thought he could build an airplane and fly Elena close enough to the sun that the radiation would heal her. He constructed his flying machine out of spare airplane parts. When it was ready, he opened her coffin and was shocked to see that his efforts to preserve Elena had failed. Her corpse was lying in a puddle of putrid, green slime. Rotting flesh barely covered her bones. Elena was almost unrecognizable!

Again, to Count Carl, this was only a minor setback.

He set out to restore Elena, to make her beautiful again. He used wires to hold her bones in place and he used wax to reconstruct her body and face. He built a wig for her out of patches of her own hair, which had fallen out when she was sick. He stuck shiny glass eyes into her empty eye sockets. And he dressed her in a wedding gown to celebrate their union.

Seven years passed. Time flies when you're in love!

Eventually Count Carl von Cosel was arrested and Elena's body was buried in a secret grave somewhere in

Key West, where he would never find it.

Years later, when the poor, persistent, love-struck count died, his neighbors found him lying on the floor beside a plaster image of Elena Milagro Hoyos Mesa, his dream love. They were together at last!

Hope you enjoyed my romantic tale. ;)

Thine in weirdness,

Diana

Chapter #8
The Blue Hole of the Pine Barrens

Remember Mrs. White? She's the old lady who lives near my grandparents and I thought she looked like a ghost because she always walks up and down the street, dressed in white.

Well, the last time I was in Leisureville, I met her. I was outside getting ready to leave and she came up to me and introduced herself. Now I know she's *definitely* not a ghost. She talks too much!

She asked me about the lights and beach umbrellas in my grandparents' backyard and I told her all about my grandfather's search for the Jersey Devil. I thought she'd think it was weird, but instead, she got excited.

"The Jersey Devil of the Pine Barrens!" exclaimed Mrs. White. "I've never met a horse-faced, flying dragon before, but I'm sure that it has its good sides. It's probably just another misunderstood monster like King Kong or Frankenstein. Ah, yes, *Frankenstein!* I remember the first time I ever saw that movie. That scene by the lake with the creature and the little girl! I wouldn't go near the water for years afterward! Do you like to swim?"

"Uh, sure," I said. I was having a hard time following the conversation. "I like to swim, I guess."

"I remember we had a dog named Trixie. She loved to swim more than anything in the world, but she used to bark at nuns, which was always embarrassing. My late husband and I never had children, but we had hundreds of pets. Dogs. Hamsters. Rabbits. Turtles. Lizards. Spiders. We even had a pet cockroach named Steve—a rhinoceros cockroach as big as your hand. Have you ever held a rhinoceros cockroach?"

That's Steve. Yuck!

Whew! People say that *I* talk fast, but Mrs. White could change the subject five times before I could complete a sentence!

But she was really nice and funny, and I thought it was cool that she once had a giant pet cockroach named Steve. Also, she seemed interested in the Weird Club.

"I used to have a weird club," Mrs. White announced. "Actually, it was a knitting club, but none of us knew how to knit. Our sweaters were awful! Unwearable!"

She glanced at her watch and her eyes went wide.

"Alrighty, it's time for me to skedaddle!" she said, heading past me down the street. "I walk fifteen miles a day and I'm behind schedule."

She stopped suddenly.

"Ah! But there's one thing I should warn you about. If your grandfather's going to be traipsing around in the woods searching for the Jersey Devil, he better watch out for the Blue Hole!"

"The Blue Hole?" I asked.

"That's right," replied Mrs. White. "It's a bottomless pool of water, and they say that if you go swimming there, it'll be the last swim you'll ever take."

The Blue Hole

She winked at me, smiling. Then she turned and walked away.

As soon as my dad and I got back to Basking Ridge, I met Mark B, and I told him about my talk with Mrs. White.

"Do you think she was serious?" he asked. "I mean, it sounds farfetched, right? A bottomless pool in the woods behind your Grampa's house?"

"I don't know," I replied. "Let's check it out on my computer."

We raced up to my room to do a search. Then we munched popcorn and read about the mysterious Blue Hole.

The Blue Hole is almost a perfect circle, about 130 feet across. That's big! The water inside it is deep blue and freezing cold, and it stays chilly all year long, even in the summer.

Why is there a round ice pool in the middle of the woods in the Pine Barrens? Mark B and I took turns searching online for the answer. There's a rumor that it's a pit made by a prehistoric meteorite. But no one really knows.

I read that birds are unnaturally silent near the hole, and the water is completely still, without any ripples or movement at all. This often tempts people to take a dip. Big mistake!

There are tales of sudden whirlpools that pull unlucky swimmers down into the depths of the bottomless hole. In other

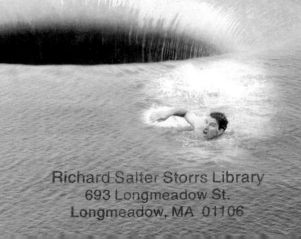

stories, the Blue Hole is not bottomless at all. It has a bottom made of quicksand. If you touch the ground, you'll get sucked under, never to be seen again.

Then I found the creepiest legend of all. It's my favorite, because it involves the Jersey Devil. According to this story, the Jersey Devil likes to use the Blue Hole as a bathtub. Some of the local townspeople believe that if you're crazy enough to go swimming in the Blue Hole, then the monster will grab you by the ankles and yank you under the water.

"Like a little rubber ducky!" added Mark B, giggling.

"It's not funny," I said. Still, I couldn't stop myself from giggling along.

But that night I thought about my grandfather, wandering in the woods in the dark looking for monsters. I didn't like the idea of Grampa becoming a bath toy for the Jersey Devil, so I wrote him a long email. I told him about the Blue Hole and what might happen if he fell into it. I told him about the whirlpools, the quicksand, and the Jersey Devil.

I got a really short email back from him a few hours later:

```
To: MarkA@weirdclub.com

I won't fall in the Blue Hole.

Love,
Grampa
```

Chapter 9

A Shoe Tree Grows in Basking Ridge

Earlier this week, my father took a business trip to San Diego, California. When he got back, I asked him what he was working on there.

"Does it involve genetic mutations?" I asked. "Nuclear warheads?"

As usual, he wouldn't reveal any information about his work. But he did tell me about something weird that he saw there. He even took pictures for the Weird Club journal.

The Shoe Tree in Balboa Park

DAD SAID that in Balboa Park there's a popular Frisbee golf course called Morley Field. (If you've never played Frisbee golf, it's kind of like playing golf with a Frisbee. I guess that's pretty obvious.) On the course, there's a big eucalyptus tree. The tree's dead, and there are no leaves dangling from its branches. Instead, there are lots and lots of shoes. Hundreds of them. All shapes and sizes.

The first pair of shoes was tossed in the tree sometime in the early 1980s. Supposedly, someone got a hole-in-one and threw their shoes in the tree to celebrate. Since then, more and more people have decorated the tree with their cleats and sneakers.

According to the story, San Diego city administrators once decided to cut down the dead tree. But a Frisbee golf player organized a protest. The city received so many angry letters and phone calls that they decided to let the "Shoe Tree" stand.

AFTER DAD TOLD ME about "The Shoe Tree of Balboa Park," I wondered if there were any other famous shoe trees. So I searched "shoe tree" on the internet and I got so many hits I couldn't read them all. There are shoe trees everywhere.

I called Mark B and told him about it. He didn't get it at first. "Why would people want to toss their shoes up into trees?" he asked.

"Maybe they do it because it makes no sense, because it's such a weird thing to do," I said. That seemed logical to him. So we decided to make a shoe tree right here in Basking Ridge!

We talked about what kind of tree would make a good shoe tree.

"It has to have lots of branches," I said.

"And the branches have to be high up off the ground, out of reach," Mark B added. "We don't want shoe thieves stealing our shoes."

That afternoon, Mark B and I rode our bikes to Lord Stirling Park. We pedaled all around the park until we found the perfect tree. I took a picture of it so we could remember what it looked like when it was shoeless.

This tree needs shoes!

Now we needed shoes, and lots of them. We decided to ask Mrs. Fishetti if we could make an announcement in homeroom. I hoped it would go better than last time.

"Mark and Mark have an announcement to make," Mrs. Fishetti said in homeroom the next day. "They're working on a fun project, and I'm sure that you'll all want to get involved! Go ahead, Mark."

Standing next to me at the front of the class, Mark B started panicking.

Trembling, he whispered to the teacher, "Uh . . . which Mark do you mean?" he asked. "A or B?"

"It's alright, I'll make the announcement," I said.

Mark B nodded. He was too shy to face the other kids, so he stared down at the gray tile floor while I did the talking. I spoke quickly because I was so nervous.

"We're the Weird Club," I said. "The purpose of our club is to look for anything that's unusual or remarkable, mysterious, unexplainable, or just plain weird!"

I heard a boy snicker at the back of the classroom. Someone else groaned.

"And . . . well, as Mrs. Fishetti said, we have a project that I think you'll all find really . . . a lot of fun! Don't you think so?" Grinning, I turned to Mark B. He forced a smile onto his face, but it wasn't very convincing.

"We're going to make a shoe tree!" I announced. "Right here, in Basking Ridge!"

The class was silent.

"Mark, I don't think anyone knows what a shoe tree is," said Mrs. Fishetti.

"It's just a tree," I replied, "with shoes hanging from it. You see, there are shoe trees all around the country. In North Carolina, Nevada, and Indiana! In Arkansas, Maine, Michigan, and New York! They're everywhere!"

Excited, I showed them a picture of the shoe tree in San Diego. I gave directions for how to find our shoe tree in Lord Stirling Park. Then I asked if anyone would like to meet us there after school to hang shoes on the tree.

Everyone stayed quiet. No hands went up.

Later, in the lunchroom, Mark B and I heard Wendy Williams talking to her friends.

"A shoe tree!" she laughed. "Why would anyone want to hang their shoes in a tree? It makes no sense!"

"Exactly!" I interrupted. "That's the reason to do it. Because it makes no sense! Because it's such a dumb idea!"

"Sounds like weirdo club logic to me," she said, rolling her eyes.

Of course, Wendy had no idea what I was talking about. And the other kids didn't either.

"They just don't get it," Mark B said. "It's okay. We can make a shoe tree without their shoes."

After school, I went home and found a pair of winter boots that didn't fit anymore. Then I rode my bike to the shoe tree to meet Mark B.

When I got there, he was sitting at the foot of the tree, looking bummed. "My Mom's giving all my old shoes to my cousin," Mark B sighed. "But she said I could hang these."

Mark B's flip-flops

He held up a pair of flip-flops tied together with string.

"Sorry," he muttered. "They're lame."

"No, they're perfect!" I said. "Let's put them in the tree."

Mark and I took turns throwing the flip-flops into the tree. That part was easy. Getting them to stay up there proved to be much more difficult. It was a windy day and the flip-flops kept flying off in the wrong direction. My boots were also hard to hang. I tied the laces together and flung them up in the air, but I missed and they almost hit me on the way back down. We realized that different footwear required different hurling techniques.

With flip-flops, you had to catch the wind just right. But with heavier shoes, it was brute force, trial and error.

Finally, the boots caught. Then the flip-flops. Out of breath, Mark B and I sat down and watched them dangling from the branches above us, twisting and turning in the breeze. Our breathing sounded loud in the empty park.

"They look nice up there, don't they?" said a voice behind us.

I turned around. It was a girl from school, Stella Lo. She's Chinese American. Always keeps to herself. Sits at the front of the class.

Stella was standing next to her bike. I wondered how long she'd been watching us. She pulled a paper bag out of her bike basket and handed it to me.

"These are for your shoe tree," she said.

Inside the bag, I found a pair of pink slippers with smiling pigs on them. They were tied together with a bright red ribbon.

"They're kind of silly," she laughed.

"Not as bad as my flip-flops," said Mark B.

Stella stepped back. "Watch this. I'll get them up there. First throw!"

She eyed the tree, concentrating, and took a deep breath. And another. Then, holding onto one slipper and swinging the other in a big circle like a pinwheel, she ran toward the tree. She let go at the very last moment and gracefully lofted her slippers into the sky.

She missed the tree completely, but it was definitely an impressive performance.

"Okay, second throw!" said Stella, retrieving her smiling pig slippers from the bushes.

"Okay, third throw!" she said after another miss.

It took her 12 tries. Which was much better than Mark B and I did.

Before we left, I took a picture.

Not much of a shoe tree, but it's a start!

Oh, I almost forgot to mention something that weirded us all out. As we were riding our bikes out of Lord Stirling Park, we realized that we hadn't been alone! We spotted Ricky and Tim Solkin hiding behind some trees. We assumed that they were waiting for us to leave so they could climb up the tree and steal the shoes. But the next day, we came back and the flip-flops, slippers, and boots were still up in the tree. So, why were they watching us? We couldn't figure it out. You never know what the Solkin Twins are up to!

Chapter #10
Home Is Where the Art Is

Sometimes people can surprise you!

I never thought much about Stella being weird, but now that I know her better, I think she's one of the weirdest people I ever met. And, of course, I mean that as a compliment.

Besides being a good shoe-tosser, Stella's an artist. This afternoon, she showed Mark B and me her latest art project. In her garage, she's been making replicas of world landmarks out of things you find in the bathroom. She made a Statue of Liberty out of toothpaste and toothpaste tubes. And now she's sculpting a Leaning Tower of Pisa out of soap. Her work was cool and strange and it smelled good too.

Did you know the Statue of Liberty was built in 1886 and the toothpaste tube was invented in 1892?

Best of all, Stella joined the Weird Club and gave me some great stories and photos for the Weird Club journal.

HAPPY CHINESE NEW YEAR

To the Weird Club:

Hello Weird Clubbers!

Stella here! Yay for the Weird Club! And yay for Mark A and Mark B! Aren't you glad my name isn't Mark? That would be really confusing. And I wouldn't want to be a girl named Mark, anyway.

Mark A said I was an artist, but I don't know if that's true. I just love making things!

My mom and dad are okay about letting me make stuff as long as I ask their permission first. So far, they've only rejected one project: For Chinese New Year, I wanted to cover the front of the house with bumper stickers that said, "Happy Chinese New Year!"

My mom said no way. "When you get your own house, you can cover it with 'Happy Chinese New Year' bumper stickers," she said. "But in this house, we put bumper stickers on the car. And only on the bumper. Don't get crazy!"

I guess it's obvious that my kind of weirdness is not about ghosts and EVPs (though I think they're really cool). I'm fascinated by people who make their own weirdness—like a house made out of newspapers or a giant dinosaur made of rusting metal. Are they artists, or are they just weird? I think maybe they're a little of each, like me. Here are some of my favorites:

The Watts Towers

The Watts Towers have been called the single largest artwork ever created by one person. In 1921, a man named Simon Rodia bought a little piece of land in the Watts district of South Los Angeles, California. Over the next 33 years, without any heavy machinery, he built towers that shot up almost 100 feet into the sky. The only help he received was from neighborhood kids. He paid them pennies and they provided bottles, broken tiles, metal, pottery, marbles, mirrors, seashells, and anything else he could use to decorate his creation. He called it *Nuestro Pueblo,* which means "Our Town" in Spanish.

"I had in my mind to do something big and I did it," he once said.

He sure did!

The Paper House

For 20 years, between 1922 and 1942, a man named Elis Stenman used old newspapers to build The Paper House in Rockport, Massachusetts.

A house made of paper???

Well, not entirely. . . . The frame, floor, and roof are made of wood. And there are normal shingles on the roof to keep the rain out. But almost everything else in The Paper House is made of old newspapers—about 100,000 of them! The walls are made out of newspaper "logs" which are 215 pages thick. And the furniture is made of newspaper, too. Mr. Stenman made newspaper lamps, tables, chairs, desks, and bookcases. He built a newspaper grandfather clock and a newspaper piano. Actually, it's a regular piano covered with newspaper. (Come on, he had to cheat a little!)

A paper piano, dining room table, and chairs!

READ ALL ABOUT IT!
Amazing house built out of 100,000 newspapers
... And so is the furniture

WHAT A PAD — OF PAPER! House is built en[tirely] except for frame, floor and chimney. Vivian [ ] niece, plays on paper piano in living room. A[ ] clock, made up of tightly rolled papers.

House. "The rods were as strong and sturdy as wood."

In 1924, Stenman hired a carpenter to erect a frame of a house, with a wood floor and a brick fireplace — then sent him home. Stenman began filling in the frame with his handmade rods and wallboards, which he made by gluing 215 sheets of paper

shaped sheet[ ] make them

Using the began cons[ ] for the next work on hi[ ] Esther eve[ ] strips of ma[ ] Paper Hous[ ]

[ing them until he had a stiff [ ]ce, like a thin cane, about three-[ ]rths of an inch in diameter," said

Jurustic Park

Have you seen the movie *Jurassic Park*? It has lots of scary scenes of ferocious dinosaurs chasing people around.

The dinosaurs at Jurustic Park are much less scary. In fact, they're not scary at all—they'll probably make you laugh instead. There's the Flying Whirlysaurus, the Siamese Twin Dragon, and the Eight-headed Octanoggin Bird. There's even a hulking Attack Dragon with rotating propeller blades on its back! Most of the dinosaurs rock and sway if you touch them or if the wind blows on them, so Jurustic Park feels strangely alive.

The owner of Jurustic Park, Clyde Wynia, says that he found all of his pre-historic creatures buried in McMillan Marsh near Marshfield, Wisconsin. He's just kidding, of course.

His creations were not really made from dinosaur bones. They were built out of rusty old car parts and other pieces of scrap metal. Mr. Wynia has been creating make-believe dinosaurs in his spare time for years.

THINKING ABOUT JURUSTIC PARK made me want to create my own dinosaur, or maybe a winged creature like the Jersey Devil! I could use scrap metal and newspapers. And I'll put a car alarm in its mouth, so it'll go "Whoop-Whoop-Whoop" at night. It'll be a funky, junky, noisy "Joisy" devil!

I know, Mom, I know. . . . When I get my own house . . .

Stay weird!

Stella

Chapter #11
Don't Forget the Coral Castle!

To the Weird Club:

Greetings, Mark and Mark and Stella!

Thanks for emailing me Stella's stories about weird art. They were all great, but I'm writing because I wanted to say, "Don't forget the Coral Castle!"

The Coral Castle was built in Homestead, Florida, by a strange and lonely man named Edward Leedskalnin. His name is too long, so I'll call him E.L. for short.

In 1913, E.L. was 26 and was engaged to Agnes Scuffs, who was 16. He called her his "Sweet Sixteen." Very lovey-dovey.

But she called off the
wedding, and the poor
guy just never got over it.
He moved to Florida and,
for 28 years, working
only at night, he built a
stone monument to his
lost Sweet Sixteen.

The Coral Castle is like a palace made out of 1,100 tons of coral
stone. There's a half-ton, heart-shaped table. *Ripley's Believe-It-Or-
Not!* called it the "world's largest valentine." There's a nine-ton

swinging gate and a 30-ton tower for
stargazing. There's even a bedroom
with twin stone beds—one for E.L.
and one for the girl who rejected him.
Doesn't that break your heart?

The weirdest part is that no one
knows how one man, working alone,
could have moved and carved these
gigantic boulders. Did he have super-
human strength? And why did he only
work at night?

The theories get pretty wacky and there are a lot of them.
Some people believe that E.L. had unraveled the mystery of how
the ancient pyramids of Egypt were built. Some say he could move
boulders by placing his hands on them and chanting. Others insist
that he had UFOs assisting him.

I have my own theory, which doesn't involve space aliens or supernatural powers. But then again, I'm a romantic kind of girl. I think that the power of love can do amazing things!

Thine in weirdness,

Diana

P.S. Hey, Mark A, I almost forgot the most important part. In this package, I'm including a pair of ballet slippers for your shoe tree. They're too small for me now, and I thought they'd look nice hanging next to your big old smelly boots. I hope you don't have too hard a time hanging them.

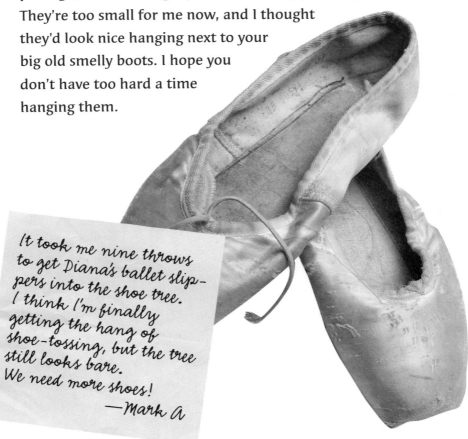

It took me nine throws to get Diana's ballet slippers into the shoe tree. I think I'm finally getting the hang of shoe-tossing, but the tree still looks bare. We need more shoes!

—Mark A

While we're talking about weird art, I just wanted to mention that San Antonio, Texas, has a weird artist named Barney Smith. He used to be a plumber, but he switched from fixing toilets to decorating them. He paints on toilet seats and glues objects to them (like license plates, eyeglasses, deer antlers, and dead yellowjacket wasps). He's created over 700 masterpieces of toilet art, and they're all on display in his garage. So, don't forget about Barney Smith, the Picasso of the potty!

—Mark B

Chapter #12
A Mysterious Letter Arrives

This afternoon, Mark B and Stella came over for the weekly Weird Club meeting in my room. I was hoping we'd spend the afternoon on my computer searching for stuff about the Jersey Devil. I had talked to Grampa on the phone last night, and he was sounding pretty fired up.

"If the Jersey Devil is out there, we'll find it!" Grampa had exclaimed. "That's our organization's motto."

"Your organization?" I said.

"Sure," he replied. "You have the Weird Club. And I have the LJDRO—the Leisureville Jersey Devil Research Organization. So far, it's just me and Mr. Bice."

At that point, my dad took the phone from me and started lecturing Grampa about not doing anything dangerous. But I knew there was no way Grampa would give up on the hunt now.

I was excited to tell Mark B and Stella all about it. But the meeting didn't go as planned. Instead, this week's Weird Club meeting was particularly . . . weird.

Leisureville Jersey Devil Research Organization

IF THE JERSEY DEVIL IS OUT THERE, WE'LL FIND IT!

It started late because my little sister Rachel wouldn't get out of my room.

"It's a Weird Club meeting," I told her. "And you're not in the club."

"Yes, I am!"

"No, you're not!"

"Yes, I am!"

It went on and on. The last thing I needed was my little sister in the club. Everything scares her. She would start to cry, and then I would get in trouble for it. Eventually, I got her out of my room and locked the door. Then we tried to begin the meeting, but there was a knock.

"What now?" I thought. "Is this meeting ever going to start?"

It was my mom. I unlocked the door and she handed me an envelope.

"This was in the mailbox," she said. "It must be for you because it's really weird."

The envelope had strange writing on it. I couldn't understand a word.

"What does it say?" asked Mark B.

"I don't know," I said. "It looks like gibberish."

"I can read it!" shouted Rachel, running back into my room.

Ugh!!!!

She grabbed the envelope out of my hands and backed up against my dresser.

To the Weird Club,
From Sasquatch

69

"I think it looks kind of backwards," Rachel said.

"Give it back!" I yelled. "You're not even in the club!"

"Yes, I am!" she insisted.

"No, you're not!"

"SASQUATCH!" shouted Stella, suddenly.

Everyone stared at her. "Sasquatch?" I repeated. It seemed like a pretty random thing to say.

Stella was looking in the dresser mirror behind Rachel. "Mark, your sister's right," Stella continued. "It's backwards. It says, 'To the Weird Club, From Sasquatch.' Look!"

We gazed at the envelope in the mirror and saw that the reflection of the handwriting was perfectly legible.

"It's mirror-writing!" exclaimed Stella.

"I knew it was," Rachel bragged, smiling up at Stella like they were best friends.

"'Sasquatch' is another name for Bigfoot," I said.

"Who's that?" asked Rachel.

"Bigfoot monsters are like giant apes. They walk like humans," I told her.

"I don't really believe they exist," said Stella.

"I do!" exclaimed Mark B. "I heard they're tall and have humongous feet. They smell bad. And sometimes they eat little kids!"

"They eat kids?" whispered Rachel, growing nervous. (See? I told you she gets scared easily.)

I opened the letter and pulled out a pencil drawing of a snarling, angry Bigfoot. "Look, there's a picture!"

Rachel shut her eyes. "No! I don't want to see Bigfoot!"

"Come on," I said. "It's only a drawing."

"No!" she shouted. Then she started crying.

So Rachel wants to join the Weird Club, but she can't even look at a drawing of Bigfoot. Like I told you, Rachel is the biggest crybaby ever.

Anyway, Rachel left. Finally! Once she was gone, we all tried our hand at mirror-writing. Here's what we wrote:

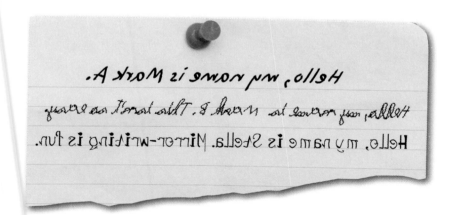

Mirror-writing is hard! But mirror-reading is much easier. We held the letter up to the mirror, and then copied down what we saw. Here it is:

To the Weird Club:

Congratulations, Weird Club, on cracking my code! That solves one mystery, but there are plenty more to keep you busy.

Who am I? And why am I writing to you?

I'm not ready to answer the first question, so let me address the second. I'm writing because your club reminded me of what I was like when I was your age. My favorite hobby was hunting for monsters. I watched a lot of horror movies back then, so I had a constant supply of terrifying monsters to search for. But there was one that intrigued me more than all the others: Bigfoot!

I was obsessed with Bigfoot. I would go on expeditions hoping to spot the creature. Of course, I didn't travel far. I just roamed around in the woods a bit. But still, the sense of mystery was exhilarating and terrifying.

For Halloween, I'd dress up as Bigfoot. I even made up a language of whoops and grunts so that I could talk like Bigfoot. (This got me in trouble at school since no one could understand what I was saying.)

Why was I so interested with Bigfoot? How can you not be

impressed by a legendary beast that stands over 8 feet tall, weighs more than 300 pounds, and has shaggy hair, broad shoulders, enormous feet, and an unbearable odor? Also, I was a shy kid and I related to Bigfoot because I thought that it was shy too. I imagined that it was a friendly creature, just very reclusive and bad at sports (like I was).

I used to always read about scary Bigfoot sightings in Washington State, Ohio, Illinois, and Pennsylvania. Unfortunately, I didn't live in any of those places. I lived in New Jersey.

"BIGFOOT in New Jersey?" I exclaimed, putting down the letter for a moment. "I wonder if we have any Bigfoot monsters in Basking Ridge!"

"I dunno," muttered Mark B. "I haven't seen any, but I just moved here."

"I'm still wondering who Sasquatch is," said Stella. "Sounds like an adult, don't you think? Maybe it's your mom. She gave us the letter, after all."

"Or your dad?" Mark B suggested. "He's kind of mysterious, isn't he?"

"I don't think it's my dad or my mom," I said. "But how can we find out for sure?"

Mark B noticed that Stella's mirror-handwriting had the same squiggles and curlicues as her regular handwriting. I ran downstairs to get samples of my parents' handwriting, and we looked at them in the mirror to see if they matched. Not even close. I didn't bother testing my older sister Michelle, because it's obvious that she has no interest in Bigfoot legends.

So, for now, the identity of Sasquatch is a mystery. Back to the letter . . .

BIG RED EYE

For the last 30 years, the townspeople of Sussex County in northwestern New Jersey have shared stories of a creature called Big Red Eye. Half-man and half-ape, the beast is said to have long black hair and piercing red eyes.

More than 50 eyewitnesses claim that they've seen the monster. Others report that they've heard Big Red Eye moaning in the dark forest at night. They say that the beast's hair-raising cry is deep and tortured, like the sound of a huge, hungry, starving animal.

In the 1970s, the creature's stomping ground was High Point

State Park, and I heard rumors that the park rangers had a night-marish time dealing with the situation. You try telling Big Red that the park is closed for the day!

THE WANTAGE BEAST
In 1977, a farmer in Wantage, New Jersey, had a run-in with a Bigfoot-like beast. The thing had clawed through an oak door. It ransacked the farmer's garage and killed eight rabbits, squashing some like bugs and tearing others to pieces.

The creature returned the following night, but this time the farmer was waiting with some friends. The men opened fire and the beast ran off, growling and possibly wounded.

Afterwards, local officials dismissed the Wantage beast as "an unidentified woods animal," most likely a bear. But the farmer and his friends insisted that it wasn't a bear. According to their descriptions, it was an ape-man with long brown hair and unfor-gettable, glowing red eyes.

THE BIGFOOT OF THE PINE BARRENS
Recently I've noticed an increasing number of Bigfoot encounters in the Pine Barrens of southern New Jersey. It's not surprising. This vast stretch of woodland is the perfect hideout for a reclusive animal like Bigfoot.

In 2003, a state policeman reported that a Bigfoot-type creature followed him down a road in Bass River State Forest, a wildlife preserve inside the Pine Barrens.

Then, in 2006, a hunter returned from the Pine Barrens with

another strange tale. He insisted that a mysterious creature in the woods threw sticks and stones at him. The hunter never actually glimpsed the beast, but claimed that he heard apelike noises and smelled that terrible Bigfoot smell—a mix of rotten eggs, putrid meat, sewage, and skunk musk. PEEEUUUU!

I wondered if Bigfoot had a problem with the Garden State. It's pretty here. And there are lots of nice woods to hide in! Why wouldn't he like it?

I began researching, collecting stories about local Bigfoot sightings, and I learned that Bigfoot has nothing against New Jersey, after all. If anything, the monster seems all too comfortable here.

So Bigfoot seems to be alive and well and living in New Jersey.

And I never grew out of my childhood obsession with Bigfoot. As a hobby, I study cryptozoology. That's just a scientific way to say that I'm still hunting monsters.

Your pal,

Sasquatch

CRYPTOZOOLOGY
The study of unknown or unexplained animals—creatures like Bigfoot, the Loch Ness Monster, and the Jersey Devil of the Pine Barrens!

Whoa! Back up, Sasquatch! Are you kidding? Bigfoot in the Pine Barrens? I thought those woods were the Jersey Devil's territory! I wonder what would happen if the two of them got in a fight. A stinky ape-man vs. a horse-faced, flying dragon. Which monster would win???

Chapter #13
My Grandfather's Nightmare

It's late at night and I can't sleep. I keep thinking about Grampa and the Jersey Devil.

We're here in Leisureville for Grampa's birthday. Birthdays are usually pretty normal in my family—dinner, cake, presents—but this one started out weird, and just kept getting weirder.

From the moment we got there, Grampa wasn't really interested in celebrating. All through his birthday dinner, he seemed restless. He kept glancing out the back window to check on the video equipment. Grandma had to remind him to finish eating. Then as soon as the meal was over, he abruptly excused himself and went outside. I followed Grampa and watched as he moved from camera to camera, changing tapes and checking the settings.

"We haven't spotted anything yet," he said as I helped him, "but we'll keep looking."

Grampa hopped onto the back porch. It was getting dark out, so he switched on the big lights that he'd set up. The glow made the trees in the forest look unreal, like the fake trees in a play at school.

"We?" I asked. "Do you mean the LJD . . . what was it?"

"The Leisureville Jersey Devil Research Organization," sighed Grampa. "Though right now, we're not much of an organization. Unfortunately, I'm the only member."

"What about Mr. Bice?" I asked.

"Bice!" grumbled Grampa. "Don't mention his name. Who needs that old fogey, anyway? He just slows everything down."

"What happened with Mr. Bice? I thought you two were friends."

"I'll tell you what happened. He quit the LJDRO! And do you know why? His daughter didn't like the idea of us wandering around in the Pine Barrens at night! But we're careful. We know what we're doing. We just make short treks into the forest. We never stray too far from the house."

Grampa peered into the woods, squinting hard and searching for movement. He turned to me and smiled. "Hey, Mark," he said. His eyes were gleaming. "Do you feel like taking a little walk in the woods with me?"

Did I!

I ran inside and got ready. I grabbed my Weird Club kit while Grampa put on his new, improved Jersey Devil hunting outfit. When I saw what he was wearing, I burst out laughing. As usual, he was wearing gym socks on his hands, and he had slid rubber bands around his wrists and ankles to protect against ticks. He was also wearing a plastic helmet and, using duct tape, he'd attached a flashlight to the top. It made him look like a miner. He had something strapped to his back with bungee cords, and he turned around to show me that it was a large tape recorder. It had a bulky remote control which was hanging from a string around his neck, along with his camera. And, last but not least, he was carrying a large plastic Whiffleball bat.

"You used to play with this when you were little," said

Grampa, waving the plastic bat. "I thought it might come in handy in case I ever need to protect myself."

Now, I'm not sure if the Jersey Devil would be intimidated by a Whiffleball bat, but I thought the outfit was amazingly weird— even for Grampa.

When my sisters saw Grampa, they laughed because he looked so silly, but my grandmother wasn't amused.

"I'm worried about you," she said to Grampa. "This Jersey Devil business has gotten out of hand!" She turned to my dad. "He hasn't been sleeping well because he keeps dreaming about the Jersey Devil. It's the same nightmare every time. And he's constantly wandering around in the woods at night. Those woods are so dark and cold, and who knows what's out there!"

"You don't need to worry," insisted Grampa as he stepped out onto the back porch. The bright lights around him cast an eerie glow on his face. "We'll stay on the path. And anyway, I know these woods backwards and forwards."

I suddenly felt a little nervous about heading out into the woods at night. I almost hoped Mom or Dad would tell me I couldn't go, but all Dad said was, "Stay on the path and don't wander off." And Mom said, "Come back in fifteen minutes, no more. And put your jacket on." I guess they trusted my grandfather more than my grandmother did.

Then Grampa grinned at me. "Let's go, Mark," he said, swinging his bat like a sword. "If the Jersey Devil's out there, we'll find it!"

We entered the woods. There was a narrow path for walkers and joggers, so now I knew why my parents weren't too worried. Plus, the lights

grampa's Wiffleball bat

on the back porch lit our way. Grampa whistled his favorite song, "Jingle Bells," as he always does when he goes for a walk.

As we forged ahead, the forest grew darker and darker, and the path grew narrower. We had to rely on Grampa's flashlight helmet. Soon, we could only see a few feet ahead. Nothing more.

"Grampa," I said as we pushed through the tangled branches, "Grandma said that you keep having a nightmare about the Jersey Devil. Would you tell it to me?"

"I don't know," replied Grampa. "It's scary. I wouldn't want my nightmare giving *you* nightmares."

"Come on, Grampa, I'm in the Weird Club! I'm sure that I can handle your dream. Hey, I'll record it!"

I walked right next to my grandfather and held up the

microphone of my tape player. I wanted to get every word, so I could document it for the club.

"Alright," said Grampa, "but I warned you."

He walked for a moment without speaking. It was really quiet in the woods, and our footsteps sounded loud as leaves crunched beneath our feet.

Then, softly, Grampa began telling his nightmare.

"IN MY DREAM, I'm out in the Pine Barrens searching for the Jersey Devil, just like we're doing. I'm whistling "Jingle Bells," as I always do."

Grampa whistled a few bars, to demonstrate. Then he returned to his dream. "It's nighttime and I'm wearing my flashlight helmet like I am now. I'm shining it onto the ground in front of me, looking for animal tracks on the forest floor.

"Suddenly, in the mud, I notice the footprint of a giant hoofed animal. I've never seen anything like it. I'm sure that it's the mark of the Jersey Devil!"

I couldn't help looking for footprints on the ground as Grampa paused. He smiled at me, and continued.

"Now, the legend says that the creature has two feet, so I look for a second footprint. Finally I find one, but it's ten feet away from the first. 'Ten feet!' I think to myself. 'What kind of animal makes tracks ten feet apart? How big is this thing?'

"I also find a carcass, half-eaten and mangled. It could be a deer or maybe a wolf. It's such a mess that I can't really tell. Whatever it is, it looks freshly killed, so I'm convinced that the Jersey Devil is close by. I stop whistling.

"I consider turning back, but my curiosity gets the best of me. I trudge on silently, and the mud gets deeper. It's so thick that I'm having trouble walking. But I keep going, sloshing through the woods.

"I find more tracks and I follow them to the edge of a dark swamp. Without thinking, I wade into the water. It's freezing, as cold as ice, but I keep going. One step. Two steps. On the third step, I sink until the muck comes up to my chest.

"Quicksand! I realize I'm in the Blue Hole and I'm trapped in quicksand!

"As I struggle to free myself, I accidentally let go of my bat. It floats away and I can no longer reach it.

"My flashlight helmet falls off and sinks quickly. Without it, I can no longer see anything. And, trapped in quicksand, I can no longer move.

"I'm paralyzed and blind. All I can do is listen. So I listen as hard as I can, waiting for a noise to break the silence.

"When it comes, it startles me. A deafening shriek! An angry beast screeching in the night! . . . I feel hot air rush against my face, and I hear the sound of splashing coming closer and closer."

Grampa stopped walking and looked at me. "The strangest

thing about this nightmare is that I don't feel frightened at the end. Instead, my heart is pounding, racing with anticipation. Even though I'm trapped in the Blue Hole in the dark and a ferocious creature is about to devour me, I feel exhilarated. 'Finally!' I think to myself. 'Finally, I've found the Jersey Devil!'"

Grampa looked at me and fell silent. I noticed that he was out of breath and his sock-covered hands were shaking. I shuddered.

"That's when the dream always ends," Grampa whispered. "Just before the thing shows up to eat me."

He wiped his forehead, and then, ducking under a low-hanging branch, he turned back towards the house. As I followed my grandfather through the woods, he began whistling—a very soft, slow, version of his favorite song.

And I have to admit . . . I don't think I'll ever hear "Jingle Bells" again without it giving me goose bumps!

Chapter #14
More Pine Barrens Weirdness

The next morning, before we left Grandma and Grampa's house, I ran into Mrs. White. She was just starting off on her morning walk.

"Has your grandfather had any luck on his search for the Jersey Devil?" she asked.

"Not yet," I answered. "But if it's out there, he'll find it!"

"Yes, indeed!" exclaimed Mrs. White. "I had the same attitude the last time I lost my house keys. 'If they're out there, I'll find them!' Of course, I'd left them on the kitchen table the whole time. Silly me! But of course, you can't compare the Jersey Devil to a set of house keys, can you?"

She glanced at her watch.

"Alrighty, it's time for me to ske-daddle. I'm behind schedule, once again. Tell your grandfather to be careful. We don't want him running into the White-Eyed Ghost of the Pine Barrens."

"Wait a minute, Mrs. White!" I called out. "The White-Eyed Ghost?"

Mrs. White nodded. "Such a sad story! Her husband was a sailor who died at sea, but she never stopped waiting for him. They say that she wanders the Pine Barrens at night, scaring people with her strange white eyes, and always asking the same hopeless question: 'Do you know where my husband is?' And if they don't know the answer . . . she curses them with years and years of bad luck!"

Mrs. White smiled and winked at me. "But the White-Eyed Ghost is a sweetheart compared to the Pine Hawkers!"

"The Pine Hawkers?"

"That's right!" continued Mrs. White. "The Pine Hawkers are a crazy family. They live in the Pine Barrens and they kill people with booby traps."

Another wink from Mrs. White. Why does she wink at me every time she says something scary?

AFTER OUR CONVERSATION, I couldn't stop thinking about the Pine Barrens. How could a stretch of woods in New Jersey be so jam-packed with so many different kinds of weirdness?

That night, I did a search on the internet. I typed in: "Pine Barrens" and "New Jersey" and "weird." And, of course, I got enough strange stories to keep me busy for hours.

I read about the Jersey Devil and the Bigfoot of the Pine Barrens. And I read about another beast so silly that I couldn't stop laughing. It's known as the "New Jersey Vegetable Monster."

A crazy old man once reported that he saw a creature in the Pine Barrens that looked like a man-sized stalk of broccoli. Of course, no one believed him. The tale was so absurd that people started making jokes about it. To this day, if a cryptozoologist (like Sasquatch says he is) hears an unbelievable story from an unreliable person, he'll shake his head and say, "That sounds like another 'New Jersey Vegetable Monster.'"

I wondered about the Pine Hawkers and the White-Eyed Ghost of the Pine Barrens. Do they really exist? Or were they invented by people with overactive imaginations, like the old man and his New Jersey Vegetable Monster?

For Grampa's sake, I hope they're just scary stories, and not real. The Pine Barrens has enough creepy monsters as it is!

Chapter #15
"Huh?" A Collection of Weird Photos

I don't like taking photos of people. Fake smiles and goofy poses are boring. I like taking pictures of weird random stuff—things you see at the side of the road that make you stop and say, "Huh?"

New Jersey is a great place for taking "Huh?" pictures. I always keep my digital camera close at hand in case I spot something weird. Here are some that I've taken on car rides with my family.

THE GIANT COWBOY OF COWTOWN
This one is for Mark B, so he won't feel homesick for Texas. It's a giant fiberglass cowboy. He's standing in the parking lot of Cowtown, the

87

oldest weekly rodeo attraction in the country.

And it's in New Jersey (that's pretty weird in itself). Yeee haaa!

GIANT LADY WITH A TIRE
Watch out! In front of a tire store in Blackwood, New Jersey, there stands a huge, 15-foot-tall woman. She's waving a car tire like she's about to throw it.

And what's with that hairdo?

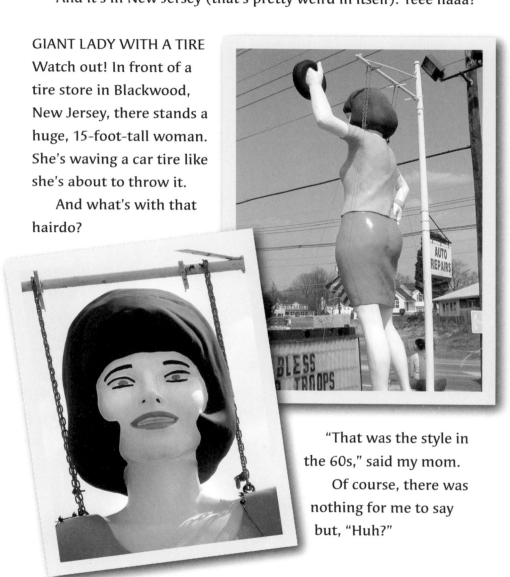

"That was the style in the 60s," said my mom.

Of course, there was nothing for me to say but, "Huh?"

WEIRD STREET SIGNS

Whenever I see a weird street sign, I always wonder who came up with the street name and what they were thinking.

For instance, was "Double Trouble Road" named after the Solkin Twins? HA!

And what kind of bummed-out sourpuss named "Life of Agony Road"? Or "Mt. Misery Road"?

My favorite weird street sign in New Jersey is this one, "Shades of Death Road." No one really knows how the road got its name. Ask around and you'll get answers ranging from ferocious wildcats to murderous bandits to fatal diseases. All I can say for sure is that I wouldn't want to live there!

When I mentioned "Huh?" pictures, it seemed like everyone I know had pictures to share as well. Take a look. . . .

GIANT COWBOY BOOTS—from Mark B:

Hey, I also like "Huh?" pictures. And it was great to see a giant cowboy in a parking lot in New Jersey.

Strange coincidence! In a parking lot in San Antonio, there's a giant cowboy who's missing. All that's left are his enormous boots. They're the World's Largest Cowboy Boots—and they're as tall as a two-story building!

Maybe the giant cowboy moved from Texas to New Jersey and forgot to pack his Justins (that's Western slang for cowboy boots).

MORE "HUH?" PICTURES—from Diana:

I've taken lots of weird "huh?" pictures here in Florida. I snapped this pic of my favorite mailbox, in a town called New Smyrna. I hope the skeleton on the motorcycle isn't the owner of the house, waiting forever for the mail to come.

Since we have the weirdest mailbox, it makes sense that Florida would also have the weirdest post office—or at least the small-est. It's in Ochopee, Florida, and it's no bigger than a tool shed.

And in Carrabelle, Florida, there's the world's smallest police station.

Only one officer can use it at a time (unless they really squeeze in).

SHIRTWOOD FOREST—from Mrs. White:

I overheard from your grandfather and Mr. Bice that you like odd pictures. Well, I have a doozy for you!

During one of my recent walks through the Pine Barrens, I spied a group of mysterious white figures with long arms, dangling in the breeze.

At first I was frightened. I thought I'd stumbled upon some kind of ghostly gang meeting, but then I realized they were shirts!

Now, who would hang dozens of white shirts near a swamp in the middle of the woods? Was it some kind of joke? Were there crazies nearby, watching me?

I didn't wait to find out. I just took a quick photo and left as quickly as possible.

Tally Ho from Shirtwood Forest! Ah, the Pine Barrens!

They just get weirder every day!

P.S. I'm enclosing a pair of old walking shoes for your shoe tree.

Jeepers! Shoe trees and shirt forests! What next? A sock bush? A pants garden? Maybe a field of underwear?

STRANGE TREES–from Stella: Hey, I was thinking about our shoe tree and I wondered what other strange kinds of trees are out there. So, I asked my uncle. He likes to travel, and he takes a lot of "Huh?" pictures wherever he goes.

Here's a picture of a bicycle-eating tree that my uncle snapped when he was in Vashon Island, Washington.

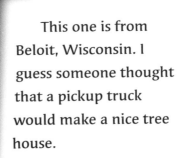

This one is from Beloit, Wisconsin. I guess someone thought that a pickup truck would make a nice tree house.

But the silliest tree from my uncle's "Huh?" collection is in Bismarck, North Dakota. It's just a

normal tree, except it's right in the middle of the road!

Pretty weird, huh? And, by the way, did you know that "HUH" in mirror-writing is still "HUH"?

Chapter #16
The Goofiest Ghost Legend Ever

While I was walking home from school yesterday, I heard footsteps behind me. I turned around and saw the Solkin Twins following me. I walked faster, but they caught up.

"Hey, Weirdo," said Ricky Solkin, stepping up beside me on the left.

"Hey, Weirdo," said Tim Solkin, stepping up beside me on the right.

"You think you're Mr. Expert on weird stuff, don't you?" said Ricky.

"You think so, but you're not," said Tim.

"Yeah," continued Ricky, "I'll bet you didn't even know that our school is haunted!"

"Really?" I asked. I didn't trust them for a minute. . . . But it would be *so* cool.

"Yeah," replied Tim. "It's the ghost of a kid named Dominick Mistrot. He was the dumbest kid in school."

"His worst subject was math," said Ricky. "His mother was driving him home from school after he flunked a math test, and she was yelling at him and not watching the road and BAM!"

"Car accident!" shouted Tim. "They both died. But Dominick's ghost still comes to school every day so he can learn math and make his super-critical mom happy. And that's why, during math class, the door to the classroom sometimes opens for no reason. Didn't you ever notice that?"

"No," I said. "I never noticed that."

"It happens all the time!" said Ricky. "That's Dominick Mistrot, coming to class late as usual."

"And sometimes when it's very quiet," continued Tim, "you can hear a ghost voice faintly whispering the wrong answers. Like if Mrs. Moyes writes '2 x 2' on the blackboard, then the ghost says, "I know! Eight! That was easy!"

"That's exactly what he says," said Ricky.

Tim nodded. "If Dominick ever gets a question right, then maybe he'll stop haunting the classroom. But it'll never happen because he's too dumb. He's wrong every time!"

Okay. That's the story the Solkin Twins told me, and they swore that it was true.

"Ask anyone!" insisted Tim.

"Yeah, ask anyone!" repeated Ricky.

TODAY'S WEDNESDAY, so we had our weekly Weird Club meeting in my room. Mark B and Stella were there, and as usual my little sister Rachel wouldn't leave us alone.

I told them all about my strange encounter with the Solkin Twins, and I asked if anyone had ever heard of Dominick Mistrot, the Math Class Ghost.

"No way," said Stella. "I think that's the goofiest ghost legend ever!"

"Me, too!" agreed Rachel, once again smiling at Stella like they were best friends. "The goofiest ghost legend ever!"

"I've never heard of Dominick Mistrot either," said Mark B, shaking his head. "And I wouldn't believe a word Ricky and Tim Solkin say. To me, it sounds like another New Jersey Vegetable Monster."

"New Jersey Vegetable Monster?" said Rachel. "What's that?"

"It just means something's an unbelievable story from an unreliable source," explained Mark B. "Because once, some old guy said he saw a giant broccoli man in the Pine Barrens."

"A giant broccoli man?" said Rachel, her eyes wide. "But the Pine Barrens are right behind Grandma and Grampa's house."

"Don't worry," I said. "The Jersey Devil will probably eat the Vegetable Monster before it will ever bother Grandma and Grampa." Rachel's face went pale. Then (big surprise!), she started crying.

"I'm afraid of the New Jersey Vegetable Monster!" she sobbed.

"Oh, come on!" I groaned. "It's not even scary!"

"It is to me!" Rachel wailed. "I HATE broccoli!"

The New Jersey Vegetable Monster!!!

Then she ran from my room in tears.

My mother called out from the hallway. "Mark, what did you do to your little sister?"

"Don't ask," I replied. I shut the door and locked it so that we could continue with our meeting.

The question before the Weird Club was: What do we do about the case of Dominick Mistrot? Should we ignore it? Or should we investigate it?

We took a vote and the decision was unanimous. We agreed that the legend of the Math Class Ghost was ridiculous and most likely a hoax, but it was our duty as paranormal researchers to investigate it.

"Besides," said Mark B. "How can we pass up a chance to ghost-hunt at our own school?"

Vegetable Monster Update

I can't believe it! Rachel has become obsessed with the New Jersey Vegetable Monster!

She keeps having nightmares about being chased in the woods by a giant broccoli man. One evening, we had broccoli with dinner, and Rachel ran from the table, crying. She even told my grampa that, while he's out in the Pine Barrens searching for the Jersey Devil, he should watch out for the terrifying and bloodthirsty New Jersey Vegetable Monster!

I can't believe she picked such a silly, stupid thing to be scared of. Ugh!!!!

Chapter #17
In Search of the Math Class Ghost

In *Dracula* movies, to keep vampires away, people always hang garlic outside their houses. I decided to hang a large stalk of broccoli outside my bedroom door to keep my little sister from invading our next Weird Club meeting.

"What is that?" asked my older sister Michelle, as I hung my broccoli man.

"It's the New Jersey Vegetable Monster," I replied. She

watched as I drew a face on it with a Magic Marker. I gave it angry eyes and sharp teeth.

"Why do I have such a weirdo for a brother?" she sighed.

Fortunately, my idea worked. Rachel didn't bother us once while Mark B, Stella, and I had our meeting!

During the meeting, we discussed how to gather evidence on the Math Class Ghost. "If Dominick Mistrot really does whisper in math class, but we can't hear him, then we need to get EVPs," I reasoned. "We need a tape recorder to capture the Electronic Voice Phenomena. But we can't just walk into class with a tape recorder."

"Why not?" asked Stella. "We can tell Mrs. Moyes that we're doing paranormal research."

"You don't know Mrs. Moyes," I said. "She once caught me trying to record the ghost of Phareloch Castle during a photography club trip. Boy, was she mad! She doesn't believe in paranormal research."

Mark B nodded. "He's right. If we want to bring a tape recorder to math class, we have to sneak it in."

I came up with a clever plan inspired by my grampa. I decided to strap the tape recorder to my back. I could wear a bulky winter coat and slide the microphone down my sleeve, so no one would notice it.

"If you wear your hood up," Mark B added, "then you can secretly listen with an earphone jack and make sure that you're recording."

"Good idea!" I exclaimed.

"I don't know," said Stella. "Don't you think you'll stand out wearing a bulky winter coat in math class?"

"Don't worry," I assured her. "People already think I'm weird. So I should dress weird, right?"

"Why are you wearing your winter coat?" asked Michelle as we left for school the next morning. "It's nice out."

"I'm smuggling my tape recorder into math class," I admitted, "so we can capture EVPs of Dominick Mistrot, the Math Class Ghost."

Then I ran off before she could say, "Why do I have such a weirdo for a brother?"

In the boys' room before Mrs. Moyes' class, Mark B helped me get ready while Stella stood guard outside in the hallway.

Mark B switched on the recorder. "Testing 1, 2, 3," he said into my coat sleeve.

I heard him in the monitor loud and clear. We were recording!

CLASS STARTED. Mrs. Moyes took attendance while I reviewed my math homework, trying to be casual. So far, so good.

Then Mrs. Moyes approached the blackboard. "5/16 + 2/3," she said, writing out the problem on the blackboard. We were learning fractions.

As she calculated the common denominator, I concentrated hard, listening to the sounds of the classroom through the monitor of my tape recorder. I was hoping to hear a spooky voice whispering a wrong answer, but all I heard was the "click-clack" of the chalk on the blackboard.

Suddenly, the monitor went dead. I slipped my hand under my hood and pressed the earphone jack harder against my ear. Still nothing. The machine was no longer recording.

I remembered how I had gotten my tape recorder working after the Solkin Twins smashed it on the sidewalk. All I had to do was shake it a little.

I jiggled, but the machine didn't start. I rocked back and forth but that didn't work either. Finally, I began bouncing up and down in my chair, shimmying and wiggling. I tried to be inconspicuous, but my chair was making light creaking noises.

"Mark!" Mrs. Moyes suddenly shouted.

I stiffened and gazed up at her. I didn't know what to say.

Mark B raised his hand. "Mrs. Moyes, uh . . . which Mark do you mean? A or B?"

"Mark Aldrich! Why are you dancing in your chair? Do you have ants in your pants?"

"No, I don't have ants in my pants," I answered. "I . . . I'm just shivering. It's cold in here, don't you think?"

"It's not cold in here," said Mrs. Moyes. "And take that big coat off. Do you see anyone else wearing a coat in this classroom?"

"No, Mrs. Moyes," I said, grimacing.

I glanced at Mark B and Stella. They were grimacing too, but there was nothing they could do to help.

I looked back at Mrs. Moyes and I faked a shiver. She didn't buy it.

"I'm not going to tell you again. Stand up this instant! And hang that coat in the closet!"

I got up, shuffled over to the closet and took off my coat. I was hoping that maybe Mrs. Moyes wouldn't notice the tape recorder strapped to my back. But of course she did.

"Mark, what's that on your back?" she asked.

I turned to face her. "It's a tape recorder, Mrs. Moyes," I replied.

Some kids behind me started chuckling.

Mrs. Moyes looked furious. "Is electronic equipment allowed in school?"

"No, but . . ."

I looked down at the floor while Mrs. Moyes stared at me. I couldn't think of anything that wouldn't get me in trouble, so I had to tell the truth. "I'm wearing it because of the ghost, Dominick Mistrot," I explained as quickly as I could. "He was a boy who was killed in a car accident a long time ago, and he was bad at math, so he haunts this classroom. I'm trying to get EVPs of him whispering the wrong answers."

By now, all of my classmates except Mark B and Stella were laughing. The Solkin Twins were laughing loudest of all.

"I don't want to hear another word about ghosts and ESP!" snapped the teacher.

"E-V-P," I corrected her. "It stands for 'Electronic Voice—'"

"Just take that thing off!" interrupted Mrs. Moyes. "Take it off and go directly to the principal's office!"

Surrounded by giggling kids, I unstrapped the tape recorder and headed toward the door. As I passed the Solkin twins, Ricky whispered, "Weirdo." Then Tim stuck his foot out and tripped me.

I fell down and my recorder smashed on the floor. Mrs. Moyes was facing the blackboard, so she didn't see them do it. As she turned around and glared at me, I gathered together the pieces of my broken machine.

I WENT to Mr. Alpert's office and sat there until the period was over. It wasn't so bad. Mr. Alpert bawled me out for bringing my tape recorder to math class, but then I was surprised because he helped me fix it. He showed me how to glue some pieces back in place, and we used rubber bands to stop the batteries from falling out.

We tested it and, on playback, my voice sounded deep, low and garbled. But at least the tape recorder still worked. Kind of.

Chapter #18
The Perfect Place for a UFO Landing

I got an email from Grampa this morning. It was very short, as usual.

```
To: MarkA@weirdclub.com

Video cameras picked up something strange.
Thought you might be interested.

Love,
Grampa
```

Two pictures were attached, still photos taken from the video. Excited, I clicked on the photos to open them, hoping to spot the Jersey Devil or Bigfoot hanging out on my grampa's lawn.

At first, I was bummed. No Jersey Devil. No Bigfoot.

But then I noticed a white light floating above the trees, in both photos. When I compared the two photos side by side, I realized that the light had moved. What could it be?

I emailed them right away to Mark B and Stella. Mark replied a half second later, "It's a UFO!"

Stella was on her computer too. After a few minutes, she replied as well. "Maybe, maybe not," said her email. "It might be a plane."

Later on, during study period at school, we met in the library to search online for news of other weird sightings in the area.

I told the librarian, Mr. Gordon, that we were researching the history of the New Jersey Pine Barrens.

"Make sure you read up on the cranberry bogs," advised Mr. Gordon. "New Jersey ranks third in the country for cranberry harvesting, and it's all because of the Pine Barrens!"

He talked about cranberries for a while, but finally he left, and we entered a search in Google: "New Jersey," "Pine Barrens," and "mysterious lights."

We found out that strange flying lights were spotted recently in Double Trouble Park near Cedar Creek. The police had received several reports about a huge circle of dead pine trees. People said that the trees were bent outward as though something had landed on them.

"They were crushed by a UFO!" declared Mark B.

"Not necessarily," said Stella. "It might have been something else."

"Like what?" asked Mark B. "A giant cranberry?"

Stella laughed. "No, silly! It might have been a meteor or a tornado–"

"Hold on, guys," I interrupted. "You're not gonna believe this!"

I clicked on an article and it came up onscreen. We all read the headline together: "SPACE ALIEN SHOT DEAD BY MILITARY POLICE IN PINE BARRENS."

According to the article, the incident happened on January 18, 1978.

The story said that UFOs were spotted over Fort Dix and McGuire Air Force Base, which are both in the New Jersey Pine

Barrens. Soon after the sightings, a military police officer noticed a strange object flying overhead. It hovered over his patrol car and then raced away. The dazed policeman pursued the UFO until suddenly a strange being appeared in front of his car. The officer got out his flashlight and saw—a skinny alien with a giant head!

The police officer panicked, pulled out his gun, and shot at the creature, wounding it. The dying alien darted away and climbed over a fence at the back of McGuire Air Force Base.

Air Force Security was alerted. A sergeant working at the base was asked to help hunt for the missing alien. He thought it was a joke at first, but he soon became a believer. On an empty runway, he and his search party discovered a dead body, and it was like no creature the sergeant had ever seen before.

Government officials in black suits arrived at the crime scene. They took over the investigation. They crated up the extraterrestrial corpse, loaded it onto a plane, and flew away. The sergeant and other witnesses were warned not to talk about the event ever again.

"Wow! My dad works for the government!" I exclaimed. "I wonder if he was involved in covering up the death of the space alien!"

"Well, one thing's for sure," said Stella. "If that story is true, then it looks like the Pine Barrens have UFOs flying over them."

"Definitely!" agreed Mark B. "Definitely UFOs!"

As if to prove the point, the next article we read said that the Pine Barrens have been called "the perfect place for a UFO landing."

Oh great! Doesn't Grampa have enough to worry about?

THAT NIGHT, I kept thinking about all the strange things I'd learned about the Pine Barrens.

I was too nervous to sleep, so I decided to email Grampa. I told him about the Bigfoot of the Pine Barrens and the murdered space alien and the multiple UFO sightings. I told him about the White-Eyed Ghost and the Pine Hawkers who use booby traps to kill people.

I was worried and I begged Grampa to be careful when he goes out at night searching for the Jersey Devil.

Grampa replied the next morning.

```
To: MarkA@weirdclub.com

I'll watch out for alien hawkers and white-eyed
bigfoots. And I won't fall in the Blue Hole.
Stop worrying.

Love,
Grampa
```

Okay, Grampa. I'll stop worrying. Or at least I'll try.

Chapter 19

Yay for Mirror-Writing!

I love mirror-writing!

Ever since we got the letter from Sasquatch, I've been practicing writing backwards. I even handed in an English essay in mirror-writing.

Mrs. Benito made me rewrite the whole thing. She thinks mirror-writing is a waste of time. "Why write backwards when you can write forwards?" she says. But I think mirror-writing is very cool.

Mirror-writing is great for writing secret messages to your friends. Of course, they'll need a mirror to figure out what you wrote. Have you ever seen mirror-writing in the real world? A lot of times, the word AMBULANCE is written backwards on the hood of the emergency vehicle. That way, when drivers up ahead look in their rear-view mirrors, they'll see the word the right way around, and they'll pull over to let the ambulance pass quickly.

And did you know that the famous artist and inventor Leonardo da Vinci was a mirror-writer? Yep, it's true! Whenever he jotted down a note to himself, he scribbled it backwards. So I say, why write forwards when you can write backwards?

Stay weird!
Stella

Hold this up to the mirror to read
—Mark

Chapter #20
A Big Pair of Clues

"The mail just came," said my mother, handing me a parcel. "Bills for me and a Weird Club package for you."

We had just started our weekly meeting. Mark B and Stella were in my room, and Broccoli Man was guarding the door, so there was no sign of Rachel.

We ripped open the package and found a note and a shoebox. The note was in mirror-writing, so right away we knew who had sent it.

"It's from Sasquatch!" exclaimed Stella. "He sent shoes for our shoe tree!" She grabbed the note and ran to my mirror.

"'Now you'll know why I named myself after Bigfoot,'" Stella read out loud. She shrugged. "What do you think it means?"

"I think I know," said Mark B, peeking in the shoebox. He pulled out a pair of men's dress shoes. Except these weren't just shoes. They were the biggest shoes I'd ever seen.

"Look at these things!" cried Mark B. "They're humongous! Gargantuan! Like boats!"

I nodded. "I guess Sasquatch has really big feet. Just like Bigfoot!"

"This is a clue!" declared Stella. "Let me think for a second. Do we know anyone who has feet this big?"

We sat in silence. Mark B raised his hand. "I knew a guy in Texas with big feet."

"Well, that doesn't really help us," said Stella, "because we're not in Texas."

"I know," muttered Mark B. "I was just brainstorming."

We decided to bring a digital camera to school the next day so that we could take pictures of men's feet. Then we ended our meeting early and rode our bikes to the shoe tree. We all took turns flinging Sasquatch's gigantic shoes into the tree. We missed every time.

Finally, a jogger passed by and asked what we were doing. I told him, and he asked if he could give it a shot. He got it on the first try. What a show-off!

Before we left, we noticed something weird. There were two new pairs of sneakers in the tree, and we had no idea who put them there. Maybe our shoe tree is catching on!

THE NEXT DAY, I brought my camera to school, and Mark B, Stella, and I took turns snapping photos in between classes all morning long. I remembered the principal's warning about bringing electronic equipment to school, so we hid behind doors, lockers, and even potted plants, and clicked away while the teachers were coming and going. No one knew that their feet were being photographed!

Here are some of the shots we took:

Mr. Togno, the gym teacher

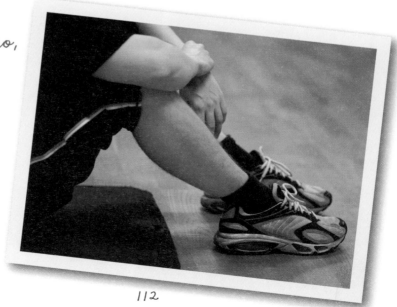

Mr. Gordon,
the librarian

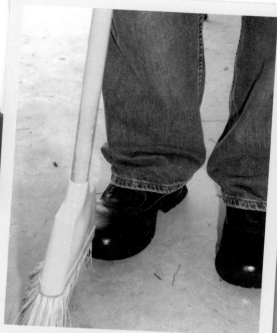

Mr. DiGiossaffatte
(Mr. D. for short), the janitor

During lunch period, we reviewed the photos together. Hiding the camera under the table, we huddled close and flipped from picture to picture. But all the feet looked normal-sized. There wasn't a Bigfoot in the bunch.

"It's hopeless!" moaned Stella. "No one has feet big enough to fit into Sasquatch's shoes!"

Suddenly, Mark B stiffened in his chair.

"Uh-oh," he whispered. "The principal is coming. You better get rid of the camera."

Nervously, I handed the camera to Stella and she passed it along to Mark B. Panicking, Mark B tossed it back to me, and I quickly hid it behind my back just as Mr. Alpert arrived.

"Mark, could you come with me?" said the principal.

Mark B raised his hand. "Mr. Alpert, uh . . . which Mark do you mean? A or B?"

The principal was looking at me. He was very serious. "I mean Mark A."

I secretly slid the camera into my back pocket and got up. Then I followed Mr. Alpert into the hallway.

"I'm afraid it's bad news," he said once we were alone. "Your mother just called the office. Your grandfather's missing."

I stared up at him in shock. I could barely speak.

"Missing?" I murmured.

The principal nodded sadly. "He went into the woods last night and he hasn't come back."

Chapter #21
An Emergency Trip to Leisureville

I went to Mr. Alpert's office and Michelle was there. She wouldn't even look at me, and I realized that she thought it was all my fault. If it weren't for me, then Grampa would never have gone into the Pine Barrens to search for the Jersey Devil. I had put the idea into his head!

"Your mother told me that the police are scouring the forest," said the principal. "They have search dogs. They even have helicopters flying overhead, hunting for signs." Mr. Alpert smiled, trying to reassure us. "I'm sure they'll find your grandfather."

"Yeah, they'll find him," I repeated. I tried to smile back, but I couldn't. I was too worried.

My mom picked us up and then we went to get Rachel. When she got in the car, Rachel was holding a fistful of tissues and crying, but for once I couldn't blame her.

My mom drove us home to meet Dad. He was standing in the driveway waiting for us, pacing nervously back and forth. I've never seen him look so fidgety. He's usually so calm and cool.

Dad climbed into the front seat, and we headed off to Leisureville. No one spoke during the trip. Rachel whimpered in the seat beside me while I gazed out the car window and watched the woods go by. I kept thinking about the Jersey Devil and the Pine Barrens with all its monsters, UFOs, Pine Hawkers, and ghosts. I kept wondering where Grampa was and whether he was okay.

WHEN WE ARRIVED at my grandparents' house, Grandma was outside, talking to a policeman who introduced himself as Officer Humphrey.

"Any news?" my father asked.

"Not really," Officer Humphrey replied. "We found some footprints, but the trail ends at a swamp."

A swamp! I remembered Grampa's nightmare and the way he described it. I imagined Grampa sinking into the quicksand of the Blue Hole with the Jersey Devil approaching.

"A swamp!" uttered my grandmother. She was unsteady and pale, sick from worrying. "What if he fell in? He doesn't know how to swim."

"Don't worry, the water was very shallow," said the policeman. "I'm sure he's alright. He just lost his way. He's out there somewhere and we'll keep looking until we find him."

Before climbing into his patrol car, Officer Humphrey told us not to go out into the woods to look for Grampa ourselves. He insisted that searchers were out there doing everything they could and he certainly didn't want anyone else getting lost.

But I couldn't just sit there and do nothing! I had to search for Grampa myself. I felt that I owed it to him. After all, maybe Michelle was right. Maybe it *was* all my fault!

I decided to sneak out at night when everyone was sleeping.

Chapter #22
The Search for My Grandfather

At midnight, I tiptoed carefully down the carpeted stairs and made sure that the coast was clear. Everyone else was in bed. Good.

I threw on a coat and sneakers and grabbed my Weird Club kit. I wanted to have my digital camera and tape recorder with me in case I ran into the Jersey Devil. Then I took a flashlight from the garage and crept out the back door, closing it softly behind me.

The porch lights were on and the video cameras were running. I walked past them toward the dark forest. As I reached the edge of the woods, I heard a whispery voice.

"Pssst. Hey . . . Hey, Mark."

It was Mr. Bice. He was standing in his backyard. I ran to join him.

"I couldn't sleep," he said. "I heard what happened to your grampa."

"I'm going to look for him," I announced.

"I'm going with you!" cried Mr. Bice. "This whole thing is my fault!"

"Your fault?" I asked.

"Yes! If I hadn't quit the LJDRO, he wouldn't have wandered off alone. We'd have gone into the forest together and he wouldn't have gotten lost!"

Hurrying as fast as he could, Mr. Bice inched toward the Pine Barrens, his walker clinking and clanking all the way.

"Now, let's move quickly," he whispered. "We have to be quiet because if my daughter wakes up, she'll stop us. She and my grandsons are visiting and she doesn't like me going anywhere near those woods."

The old man took another step. Then the porch light behind us flicked on. Mr. Bice flinched. The back door of his house opened and two boys in pajamas stepped out. They were tall with messy red hair.

I couldn't believe my eyes. They looked exactly like the Solkin Twins!

"Look, it's Weirdo!" one of them shouted.

"What are you doing in our grandfather's backyard?" said the other.

They *were* the Solkin Twins! And they looked as shocked as I was.

Mr. Bice hobbled towards them quickly. "Shhh! Or you'll wake up your mother. Mark and I are heading into the woods to look for his grampa."

"Now? In the middle of the night?" said Tim.

"I don't think so," said Ricky, backing into the house. "I'm gonna get Mom."

"Don't you dare!" barked Mr. Bice. "I'm going into those woods to look for my friend and nothing's going to stop me!"

"Then we're coming with you," said Tim.

"Yeah, we're coming with you," said Ricky.

Ricky and Tim rushed inside to grab jackets and sneakers. I was getting more and more impatient to start searching.

They reappeared a few minutes later, and we were finally about to get under way when we were hit with a flashlight beam.

Squinting into the light, we saw a figure approaching.

It was Mrs. White. She was wearing a trenchcoat and holding a compass out in front of her.

"Ah, it's you!" she said when she saw me. "I imagine you're going out to search for your grandfather."

"That's right," I replied.

"Well, I was just about to conduct my own search. I know the Pine Barrens better than anyone, but the forest can be tricky, so I brought my trusty compass. I also brought my kazoo."

She proudly presented a metal kazoo dangling from a string tied around her neck.

"What's that for?" I asked.

She grinned. "To soothe the savage Jersey Devil! I read on the Internet that wild beasts enjoy listening to music. Animals are fascinating, aren't they?"

"Um, sure," I said. I turned towards the woods and led our unusual search party into the Pine Barrens. A frail old guy with a walker, an old woman dressed all in white, and twin bullies who hated me. What a weird group we made!

Following the narrow path, I walked in front with a Solkin

Twin on each side of me. They crowded close, so I knew they were scared. Mrs. White trailed behind us, helping Mr. Bice maneuver his walker through the thick underbrush. Mr. Bice moved as fast as he could, but our progress was slow.

After 20 minutes, I could still see the bright lights on my grampa's back porch.

Another ten minutes passed and the forest grew black and threatening. As impatient as I was to find Grampa, I was also secretly relieved not to be alone in the forest.

I snapped this picture in the woods. You can see how dark it was that night!

As we shuffled into the dark, I told the Solkin Twins about the Jersey Devil.

"You mean, a horse-faced flying dragon lives in these woods?" asked Ricky. I felt him shudder beside me.

"And it has sharp claws and jagged teeth?" asked Tim. He spun around and called out to his grandfather. "Popsy, are you sure you don't want to go back? I'll go with you if you want."

"'Popsy'?" I said, trying not to laugh. "You call your grandfather 'Popsy'?"

"Yeah, he's our Popsy!" replied Ricky. "What's wrong with that?"

"You know, Mrs. White," said Mr. Bice (also known as Popsy), trudging along behind us. "I come from West Virginia, and there we had our own flying monster called Mothman!"

"Ah yes! I've heard of Mothman!" exclaimed Mrs. White. "Well, I come from Alton, Illinois, home of the giant, vicious Piasa Bird—the Bird that Devours Men!"

"It . . . it . . . it devours men?" stammered Tim.

The Dreaded Piasa Bird

"That's what they say," chirped Mrs. White. "Oh, it's a nasty monster! It eats men, women, children, dogs, even ponies! Everything it comes across."

They kept talking, but all I could think about was my grampa. Suddenly my flashlight revealed a glint of red on the forest floor. I stopped and shined the light down. Everyone else crowded around me. It was a pile of bloody fur and bones! It was just like the animal carcass in Grampa's dream!

"Wh-what is it?" gasped Ricky.

"I don't know," I said, "But I think it used to be some kind of animal."

"That's it!" howled Tim. "I don't care what you guys do! I'm going home!"

Tim lunged backwards, bumping into Mrs. White.

"Oh dear, I dropped my compass! I can't find it!" cried Mrs.

White, bending and feeling around in the muck.

"We're lost!" yelped Ricky, starting to panic.

"We're not lost," said Mr. Bice. "We're fine. Stay calm."

That's when I saw it. In the mud up ahead . . . "A footprint!" I said. "Look! A footprint!"

I shined my flashlight on the track. It was hard to see, but I could just barely make out a heel mark and three pointy toes. And it was big! Really big!

I grabbed my camera and quickly snapped a picture. My hands were trembling. "Maybe it's the Jersey Devil!" I exclaimed.

My mind started racing. I couldn't stop thinking about Grampa's dream, and I couldn't shake the feeling that if I could find more tracks, then I would find the Jersey Devil. And if I found the Jersey Devil, then I would find Grampa.

I started talking really fast. "In Grampa's dream, the Jersey Devil's tracks were ten feet apart."

I stepped forward, counting out loud, measuring the distance with my steps.

"One . . . two . . . three . . ."

"Don't go any further!" pleaded Tim.

"Yeah, it'll devour you!" hollered Ricky.

"Four . . . five . . . six . . . seven . . ."

Keeping my flashlight pointed down, I scanned the forest floor, searching for the next track.

"Eight . . . nine–"

My foot caught on a branch. I tripped and fell down with a splash. Ice-cold water hit my face.

"The Blue Hole!" I cried out.

I wriggled and shook, trying to free myself, but the mud was too thick.

Quicksand!

I dropped my tape recorder and my flashlight. The light cut off, leaving me in darkness.

"THERE IT IS!" shrieked Tim. "IT'S THE JERSEY DEVIL!"

I looked up and saw two orbs floating in the night like eyes.

"Ahhhhhhhh!" screamed Ricky.

"Stay calm," Mr. Bice kept saying. "Everyone stay calm!"

I froze.

The eyes came closer, bobbing and swaying, until I realized that they weren't eyes at all. They were flashlights!

A beam lit up the woods around me, and suddenly I realized that I hadn't fallen into the Blue Hole. I was lying in a big cold puddle of swamp water. I started laughing. I couldn't help it.

"What are you doing out here?" I heard a voice ask sternly. "I thought I told you to stay put."

I stopped laughing. It was Officer Humphrey, the policeman from Grampa's house. He reached down a hand to help me up. Another policeman stood beside him.

"I was looking for my grampa," I replied. "I couldn't just stay inside and wait! I had to–"

"We found him," the second policeman interrupted.

"Really?" I asked. "You found him? You found Grampa?"

"Yes," said Officer Humphrey, smiling. "He's home safe."

I was so excited to hear that Grampa was okay, I gave Officer Humphrey a big hug. I realized too late that I was covered in mud—and now he was too. But I was too happy to care.

"But now my grandsons are lost!" shouted Mr. Bice. "Tim! Ricky!" he called, sounding worried.

"We're up here!" someone cried from above.

"Yeah Popsy, we climbed up, but we can't get down!"

The policemen pointed their lights into a tree and, sure enough, high up in the branches were the Solkin Twins.

"Alright," said the muddy Officer Humphrey, starting to climb. "I'll get them down."

Here's what I saw in the mud. Could it be the footprint of the Jersey Devil?

Chapter #23
Grampa's Encounter in the Woods

When I got home that night, everyone was waiting for me in the living room. Mom and Dad took turns yelling at me for going into the Pine Barrens at night. Even Grandma snapped at me. I guess I deserved it.

I didn't get to talk to Grampa because they'd taken him to the hospital in an ambulance. "Nothing serious," my dad said. "He's just exhausted and frightened after being lost in the woods for so long."

We visited Grampa the next day. We all crowded around his hospital bed, telling jokes and stories about everything *except* the Pine Barrens. No one wanted to talk about what had happened.

Grampa looked fine, but maybe a little tired. He said the doctor wanted to keep him there for another day, just to keep an eye on him.

"Hey, Grampa," I announced. "I brought you a pair of gym socks to keep your hands warm."

"Very considerate of you," he replied, stuffing his hands into the socks.

"Take those off your hands," said Grandma sharply. "It's one thing to look ridiculous at home, but this is a hospital!" She tried to look stern, but I noticed that she had a tiny smile on her face. I was glad to see Grandma smiling again.

All through our visit, Grampa kept looking at me like he wanted to tell me something. Finally, as we were about to leave, he said, "Listen, Mark, can I talk to you alone for a minute?"

"Sure."

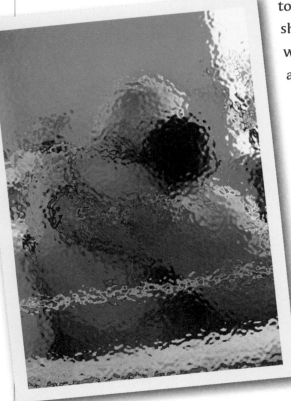

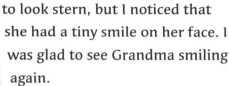

Here's a cool photo my mom took of me and Grampa in the hospital. Taken through a rippled glass window in the door to his room.

"Don't talk too long. Your grandfather needs rest," said my father.

Grampa waited as my family cleared out of the room.

"I didn't want them to hear this. They'll think I'm crazy, but you'll believe me."

"I'll believe what?" I asked.

"I saw it," he whispered. "I saw the Jersey Devil."

I sat on the edge of the bed, and said, "Tell me! Tell me everything!"

And he did.

"I WENT OUT that night searching for the Jersey Devil," Grampa began. "I wandered around for hours before I realized that I was lost. Maybe I knew it sooner, but I didn't want to admit it. I kept hoping I'd find the path that would lead me home.

"Finally, I couldn't walk anymore. I needed to rest. I found a nice soft pile of leaves, and lay down in them. I started whistling to keep my mind off the fact that I was lost."

"'Jingle Bells'?" I asked.

"Of course. What else am I gonna whistle?"

Grampa closed his eyes and then opened them again. "I blinked just like that. I closed my eyes, but only for a second. And when I opened them a terrifying creature was hovering over me, fluttering its wings!"

"The Jersey Devil?" I whispered.

Grampa nodded. "It was a whole zoo in one animal, just like you said, Mark. Every part of it seemed to come from a different

creature. Horse's face. Kangaroo body. Human legs. Deer antlers. Long, pointed dragon tail. And enormous bat wings. The wings were absolutely spectacular. They seemed to fill the sky!

"You can't imagine how big it was!" Grampa shouted from his hospital bed. "It was bigger than an elephant! Bigger than a house! How could something that big be so hard to find? . . . But you know what the weirdest thing was?"

I shook my head. I couldn't say a word. I was too stunned.

"It was glowing in the dark like a colossal firefly! Unbelievable!" Grampa gazed up at me and smiled, remembering. "It stared at me for a while and I stared back, clutching my bat. It's like we were trying to figure each other out.

"Finally, I came to my senses. I realized that no one was going to believe that I had actually seen the Jersey Devil. I needed evidence, so I decided to snap a picture. I grabbed my camera, lifted it to my eye. And . . . nothing. Everything was black!"

Grampa smacked himself in the head with his hand. "Oh, I was such a dummy! The lens cap was still on! If only I had been better prepared!"

Grampa sighed and leaned back against his pillow. "There's nothing more to say. I took the lens cap off, but when I looked through my camera again, the Jersey Devil was gone."

MY GRANDMOTHER asked us to stay one more night in Leisureville. I could tell she wanted the company until Grampa came home the next day.

After dark, I sat on the back porch and thought about what Grampa had told me.

I have to admit, his story freaked me out. I didn't know what to think. Was it all in his imagination? I mean, he was tired and hungry, right? Maybe his mind was playing tricks on him. Or maybe he fell asleep in those leaves and dreamed it all.

But what if it all really did happen exactly as he described it? What if my grampa really did come face to face with the Jersey Devil? If the monster really glowed in the dark, that could explain the weird, traveling light in the photos that Grampa had sent me. Maybe the UFO in those pictures was actually the Jersey Devil!

These strange thoughts bounced around in my brain until my head started to hurt.

Rachel came outside and plopped down beside me on the porch. We sat there silently for a few moments.

"Grampa said he saw it out there," I told her.

"Saw what?" asked Rachel. "The New Jersey Vegetable Monster?"

"No, the Jersey Devil."

"Oh," said Rachel. "I thought maybe he saw Broccoli Man." She sounded disappointed.

We sat together, peering into the Pine Barrens and imagining the monster that might be out there. We weren't thinking about the same monster, but that didn't really matter.

Rachel usually gets on my nerves, but that night I was glad she was there with me. I was feeling pretty creeped out and I'm sure that Rachel was too. So we leaned against each other, shoulder to shoulder, and it made me feel a little better.

Chapter #24
The Weird Club Becomes Official!

A lot has happened since my last entry.

First of all, we drove back to Basking Ridge. In the car, on the way home, I realized that I didn't have my tape recorder.

"Oh no!" I cried. "I left it in the woods! I dropped it when we were searching for Grampa, but there was so much happening that I forgot to pick it up!"

Even though it was mostly broken, I was really disappointed.

"Well, we're not going back to find it," said my dad.

THE NEXT DAY, the Solkin Twins caught up to me on the way to school. I wasn't sure what to expect, but I knew I wasn't scared of them anymore.

"Hey, Weirdo," said Ricky.

"Hey, Weirdo," said Tim.

"Don't you dare tell anyone about the other night," Ricky warned. "Don't tell anyone we got scared or that we got stuck in a tree."

"Yeah," said Tim. "And don't tell anyone that we call our grandfather 'Popsy'."

I smiled. I couldn't help it. I thought they would pound me, but to my surprise, Ricky and Tim smiled too. Just a little.

I promised I wouldn't tell anyone.

Mark B and Stella came over for our weekly Weird Club meeting on Wednesday. They asked me a million questions about the search for the Jersey Devil, but before I could answer, the doorbell rang. I answered it and was surprised to find Ricky and Tim Solkin standing on my porch.

Mark B and Stella came up behind me. The three of us stared at the Solkins and they stared back. Finally, the twins broke the silence.

"Hey, Mark," said Ricky.

"Hey, Mark," said Tim.

I had never heard them call me by my name before. It seemed kind of weird.

"This is for you," said Ricky, handing me a box. "It's a tape recorder. A brand-new one."

"Yeah," said Tim. "We chipped in and got it for you. We're sorry we smashed yours that one time."

"Twice, actually," I said. Stella elbowed me.

"Not that I'm counting," I added quickly. "Thanks!"

"No problem," said Ricky. "Also, we, uh, we wanted to, um–"

"Could we join your club?" asked Tim.

Stella, Mark B, and I looked at each other in shock. It seemed so strange that the Solkins would want to join the Weird Club. But, like I said . . . sometimes people can surprise you!

"That night in the woods," said Ricky. "We can't stop thinking about it."

"Yeah, it was awesome!" said Tim. "Scary but awesome!"

"And all that weird stuff you like," said Ricky. "Ghosts and flying creatures and stuff . . ."

"We actually sorta like all that weird stuff," said Tim. "We even hung our sneakers in your stupid tree."

"Those were *your* sneakers?" Stella laughed. "We didn't know where they came from."

Then the Solkin Twins told us that their Aunt Pearl was an antiques dealer, and she recently bought a huge collection of stuff from an old lady with a serious shoe-buying problem.

"Long story short," said Ricky. "Our aunt now has a bazillion shoes."

"And she doesn't want them," said Tim. "So she's gonna give them to us for the shoe tree."

So now the Weird Club has two new members and a bazillion shoes!

THAT BRINGS US to the BIG SHOE TREE PARTY! But first, let me tell you how the Weird Club became official.

Since we now had five members, we were big enough to be recognized as a real club at school.

The five of us met at the principal's office. Ricky and Tim were kind of nervous about being there—this was the first time they had gone there without actually being in trouble.

Mr. Alpert was sitting behind his desk and we all filed in. He raised his eyebrows when he saw the Solkin Twins with us.

"We're the Weird Club," I said to the principal. "And there are five of us now! See? One, two, three, four, five!"

"Yes, I can count," Mr. Alpert interrupted.

"You said that if we had five members, then we could be a real, official school club," I continued. "We would be mentioned in the yearbook and we'd get money from the school for expenses, and even field trips."

"Where's your faculty sponsor?"

My smile drooped.

"Our faculty sponsor?" Mark B turned to me. "You didn't say anything about a faculty sponsor."

"Well, of course, you need a sponsor," Mr. Alpert said. "You need an adult from school to supervise the club."

"Who would want to sponsor something as weird as the Weird Club?" Ricky asked.

"I think I can recommend someone," said the principal. He grabbed a pen and a sticky note. He jotted something down, and then lifted the paper to show us.

"Sasquatch!" said Stella right away.

That's right! The mysterious, mirror-writing cryptozoologist was Mr. Alpert, the school principal. And he had the big feet to prove it!

"Size 15," said Mr. Alpert, plunking his feet up on his desk. "It's not easy finding shoes."

We filled out a form and Mr. Alpert signed it as our faculty sponsor. The Weird Club was now an official school organization!

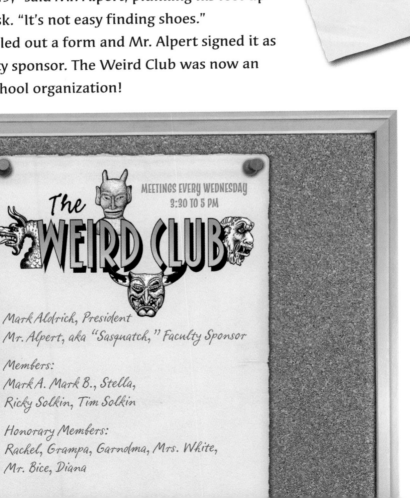

The WEIRD CLUB

MEETINGS EVERY WEDNESDAY
9:30 TO 5 PM

Mark Aldrich, President
Mr. Alpert, aka "Sasquatch," Faculty Sponsor

Members:
Mark A. Mark B., Stella,
Ricky Solkin, Tim Solkin

Honorary Members:
Rachel, Grampa, Garndma, Mrs. White,
Mr. Bice, Diana

OKAY. Now, where was I? Oh yeah, I remember . . . Our <u>BIG SHOE TREE PARTY</u>!

Stella, Mark B, and I rode our bikes to the shoe tree. Then Ricky and Tim showed up with their Aunt Pearl in a pickup truck that was *overflowing* with shoes.

We spent the whole afternoon flinging, hurling, lobbing, and tossing. Soon a crowd gathered around us to watch. A lot of people even joined in, including some kids from school. Shoes were flying everywhere and the sneakers, flip-flops, slippers, and other shoes that were already on the branches were swinging wildly. It was the funniest thing I'd ever seen.

Finally, Sasquatch—er, I mean, Mr. Alpert— came by with pizza and soda and we had a pizza party under the shoe tree.

While we were eating, a reporter came by and asked us some questions. He said he was writing an article for the local paper. A few days later, I clipped this article from the paper:

THE MOST BOOT-IFUL TREE IN LORD STIRLING PARK

Recent visitors to Lord Stirling Park may have noticed a tree bearing unusual fruit — not the kind you can sink your teeth into, but a strange blossom that you can stick your foot into instead. Yes, this odd tree seems to be growing shoes!

It's the work of a local group of kids that calls itself The Weird Club.

"Shoe trees are everywhere," said the club's leader, 12-year-old Mark Aldrich. "They're all over the country. We decided to make one right here in Basking Ridge."

"It's like a community art project," added club member Stella Lo. "Everyone can participate. All you need is an old pair of shoes."

According to club members, the Basking Ridge Weird Club is about much more than flying footwear.

So, send your stories of weirdness to Mark and the gang at: WeirdStuff@weirdclub.com.

And if you happen to pass their wonderful shoe tree, feel free to offer up your sneakers. Then enjoy the day strolling barefoot in the park.

Chapter 25
The Search Continues

Good news! The article about our shoe tree got picked up by the Associated Press. That means it was printed in newspapers around the country. Ever since then, I've been getting weird emails from all over the place.

A boy in Vermont said that his favorite hobby is hunting sea serpents.

And a girl in Hawaii told me about a haunted pond near where she lives.

I also get a lot of packages in the mail (mostly shoes). Today I got a package from Grampa! There was a note inside. I expected it to be short and sweet as usual, but it was really long, at least for Grampa:

Dear Mark,

   I just wanted to let you know that I haven't stopped searching for the Jersey Devil. Now that I've seen the thing up close, I'm determined to find it again and prove that it really exists. And the next time, I'll be ready with my camera!

   The LJDRO is going strong. Mr. Bice has joined the club again, and we have a new member, Mrs. White. We go out every evening for a walk in the woods. Don't worry, we're being very careful to stay on the path, so I won't get lost in the forest again. Besides, Mrs. White is very handy with a compass. Incidentally, I think old Bice has a crush on her. There's someone for everyone, I suppose.

   One more thing: On our last expedition, I found your tape recorder in the woods and I'm including it in this package. Something happened to it. I thought you might be interested.

   Love,
   Grampa

UNDER THE NOTE, I found my old tape recorder—or at least what was left of it. Half of it was missing and the rest was covered with dried mud and jagged dents.

   "Wow!" I said out loud. "These look like bite marks!"

Rachel was passing outside my room and she heard me.

"What's that?" she asked.

"Something chomped my tape recorder! Bit it right in half!"

I examined the demolished tape recorder with my sister. "Maybe it was the Jersey Devil," I said.

"Or maybe it was the New Jersey Vegetable Monster," said Rachel, smiling at me.

"Well, whatever it is," I declared. "If it's out there, we'll find it!"

Picture Credits

Randy Fairbanks

Randy grew up in Stanhope, New Jersey, and studied filmmaking at N.Y.U. Graduate Film School in New York City. As a writer of children's stories, he appeared regularly as Uncle Randy on the weekly radio program Greasy Kid Stuff on WFMU. Randy started his first Weird Club in grammar school. It was called the Monster Club, and he was the only member.

Mark Moran

A lifelong resident of New Jersey, Mark has spent most of his 45 years wandering the back roads and back woods of the Garden State in search of the unusual. One day, while roaming deep in the Pine Barrens, he happened upon a fork in the sandy crossroads. He chose to take the road less traveled and has never looked back.

These days Mark lives a deceptively normal-looking life in a quiet Essex County suburb with his wife and their two daughters.

Mark Sceurman

Mark was born and bred deep in the heart of the suburban wastelands of New Jersey. He has been in the publishing industry for 28 years as a graphic artist, editor, and publisher, starting with *The Aquarian Weekly* newspaper, and then set out with an adventurous magazine called *Weird N.J.*

He lives in the county of Essex with his wife and daughter. He no longer calls his surroundings a suburban wasteland, but rather prefers to see it as "Jersey rhythms."

ACKNOWLEDGMENTS

This book would not have been possible without Mark Moran and Mark Sceurman of *Weird N.J.* I'm grateful to them for having faith in me and for their tireless dedication to weirdness of all kinds. I'm also grateful to my editor, Dena Neusner; art director, Richard Berenson; illustrator, Ryan Doan; and publisher, Barbara Morgan, and to the many contributors to *Weird U.S.* who gave me so much outstanding material.

Thanks to my friends and family for their help and support. I particularly wish to thank Adam Nadler, who gave me great comments and encouragement all along the way. Also my parents, Elizabeth Applegate, Shelley and Pete Bazinet, Hillary Fairbanks, Ray Kosarin, Henry Maler, Mallory and Lance Norman, Marie Regan, and Aileen Tsui. And special thanks to Belinda Miller, Hova Najarian, and WFMU for putting me on the road that eventually led to this book.

Last but not least, my sincere appreciation goes out to all the kids who inspired this project by writing to *Weird N.J.* (especially Wildcat, whoever you are).